GOLDEN

4/2010

GOLDEN

Jennifer Lynn Barnes

DELACORTE PRESS

Published by
Delacorte Press
an imprint of
Random House Children's Books
a division of Random House, Inc.
New York

Text copyright © 2006 by Jennifer Lynn Barnes

Visit us on the Web! www.randomhouse.com/teens
Educators and librarians, for a variety of teaching tools, visit us at
www.randomhouse.com/teachers

Library of Congress Cataloging-in-Publication Data

Barnes, Jennifer (Jennifer Lynn)
Golden / Jennifer Barnes.
p. cm.
Summary: When her family moves to Oklahoma from California, high school
sophomore Lissy uses her ability to see other people's auras to try to uncover and
stop the sinister activities of a teacher at her new school.
ISBN-10: 0-385-73311-9 (trade)—ISBN-10: 0-385-90330-8 (glb)
ISBN-13: 978-0-385-73311-3 (trade)—ISBN-13: 978-0-385-90330-1 (glb)
[1. Extrasensory perception—Fiction. 2. Self-actualization (Psychology)—Fiction.
3. Moving, Household—Fiction. 4. High schools—Fiction. 5. Schools—Fiction.]
I. Title.
PZ7.B26225Gol 2006
[Fic]—dc22   2005009312

The text of this book is set in 12-point Garamond.
Book design by Trish P. Watts
Printed in the United States of America
July 2006
10 9 8 7 6 5 4 3 2 1
BVG

acknowledgments

I owe a big thank-you to three women without whom Lissy's story might never have been told. To my agent, Elizabeth Harding, whose comments and suggestions are almost invariably spot-on and whose support and kindness make the process a pleasure; to Krista Marino, editor extraordinaire, for invaluable input, never-ending enthusiasm, and a delightful willingness to help me procrastinate over classwork; and to my mother, Marsha Barnes, who suffered through cliffhangers, typos, and late-night additions and then proceeded to read no fewer than five subsequent drafts not only with love and passion, but also with incredible insight and patience, for which I am extremely grateful. I feel truly blessed to have been able to work with you all.

Thanks also to Susie Inhofe for help along the way, and to Neha Mahajan, Mariko Yamuguchi, and Bill Barnes for their comments on earlier drafts. Finally, I couldn't have done this without the nonstop encouragement and support of my family and friends. Thank you all for your enthusiasm, for the late-night pep talks, and for listening to my excited ramblings about agents, editors, covers, and revisions no less than twice per week.

To the people who helped me survive high school
without the aid of mystical Sight.
Mom, Dad, Justin, and Chelsea,
this one's for you.

1

blue

DARK.

Looking around, I saw nothing, but I could feel the wrongness of it all in the air, and the hairs on the back of my neck stood straight up. Why couldn't I see? I was blind and terrified, and the ground shook violently beneath me. The earth burst into flames, and with the heat on my neck, images raced through my mind. Three intertwining circles, rings of different colors on a silver shield. Grams and Mom, Lexie and me. Paul. Fire and colors, color and fire, even though it was still dark. Shadows and light. Shadows and light and color, and then, there was nothing.

My eyes flew open, and I gasped for air. Where was I? Why was my face squashed up against a window? Was I drooling? And who were those girls staring at me?

My mind still a mess of images from my dream, I eased my numb face off the window and quickly checked my chin for drool. Ewww. Two days trapped in a car with my family, and I was *drooling*.

"Back to the land of the living, Lissy?" my mom asked from the front seat. I would have shot her a dirty look (how hard was it to remember that I wanted to be called Felicity and not Lissy?), but I couldn't seem to look away from the window. Or, more specifically, the scene *outside* the window.

You know those mythical creatures that have snakes for hair and if you look at them, they turn you to stone with their deadly gaze? Well, the looks the three teenage girls in the car next to us were sending my way had me good and stoned, and not in a Just Say No kind of way.

The blonde in the driver's seat had this soft, sick smile on her face, and she met my eyes as if to clarify that yes, she was laughing *at* me (and my drool), not *with* me and that no, I didn't have a right to be looking back at her. I wanted to look away. I tried to look away, but the best I could manage was shifting my gaze from the blonde to the passenger seat. A girl with long, dark hair arched one eyebrow in my general direction, somehow managing to stare down at me, even though she was in a tiny convertible and I was in an SUV. Impressive.

Again, I tried to look away, but I was stone. Stone that still might have had some drool on the left side of her chin.

I turned my attention to the last girl in the car. An obvious fake blonde, she snarled at me for a full four seconds and then glanced down at her fingernails. Apparently, I was just interesting enough to merit a snarl, but not more interesting than her French manicure.

"What were you dreaming about?" Lexie's voice broke into my mind, and finally, I was able to look away from the convertible. When I glanced back a microsecond later, I'd faded from their radar, and they sped up and passed us on the left.

"Were you dreaming about Paul?"

I narrowed my eyes at Lexie, but apparently, my snarl needed a little work.

"You were dreaming about Paul," my little sister declared softly, her eyes wide and her voice sure. "Weren't you?" Lexie looked earnestly up at me, a lop-sided smile on her pixie face.

It was impossible to stay mad at my sister, even when I wanted to, much like it was completely impossible not to think about the fact that the only teenagers I'd come across so far since we'd entered this "state" had seen me with my nose pressed up against a window. What if they'd seen up my nose? As if the drool wasn't bad enough.

"Lissy? Dream? Paul?" Lexie was nothing if not persistent.

"Among other things," I muttered, casting a cautious glance in my mom's direction. She didn't know about Paul and me, if there was anything to know, and the last thing I wanted to do was spend the final leg of our car

3

ride playing the Probing Questions game. Lexie got the message loud and clear, and she didn't say anything else. I stared out my window, watching the trees and telephone poles fly by and keeping my eyes peeled for blue convertibles. After a while, the trees blurred together, I stopped wondering if anyone had seen up my nose, and I let myself get caught up in memory.

Paul Carter: next-door neighbor, partner in crime, best friend. Paul, who called me Weasel and insisted it was a term of endearment. Paul, who laughed with me, even when I wasn't funny. Paul, who had held my hand on the first day of kindergarten and sat on the beach with me after our first day of high school. Paul.

I could practically see him as he had been when our car had pulled away: standing on the beach, sand in his dark hair, his eyes locked on mine. He'd kissed me. I'd been übercrushing on my best friend, Paul Carter, ever since he'd dumped sand down my back when we were four, and right before my parents, Lexie, and I had packed our bags and moved halfway across the country, he'd kissed me. Actually kissed me. We'd meant to say goodbye then. We'd wanted to go out on a high note: s'mores on the beach and then watching horrendous science fiction B-movies, completely without any mention of the fact that I was leaving. Things had been proceeding according to plan, and then boom: he'd kissed me.

In retrospect, it hadn't been a boom at all. It was actually more of a whoosh, as my lungs collapsed and my heart stopped beating, followed quickly by an imaginary sound that I could only describe as the accordion noise cartoon characters always made after they'd been hit with an anvil.

And now, a thousand miles away from home and who knows how far from civilization, all I had left of Paul was the seashell he'd given me on my sixth birthday, his last words to me ("I'll miss you, Weasel"), and a memory of him on the beach. The colored lights around him had stood out, midnight blue against the stark white sand, moving in slow waves as he watched me drive away forever.

I bit the inside of my lip as I thought about Paul's colors. He had always been a blue, but the color had darkened as he'd grown older, until it was the color of the ocean during a storm.

I pushed the thought out of my mind. We were moving across the country so that we could start a new life, and short of willing Paul to come to Oklahoma to get me, I had only one goal. I was going to be normal, and that meant no more color vision. Turning my head away from the window and squeezing my eyes shut, I mentally forced down the part of me that saw the colored lights.

"It won't work," my mom told me from the front seat. She hadn't even had to turn around to know what I was doing. That was by far the most irritating thing about my mother. Some moms had mom sense or mom radar. My mom had something way more powerful. Nothing got past her, except, I hoped, what had happened between Paul and me, if something had really happened.

"What won't work?" Lexie asked, completely oblivious to what I'd been trying to do. My dad simply switched lanes without saying a word.

"It won't go away just because you want it to, Lis," my mom told me for maybe the hundredth time in the past two weeks.

I didn't say anything. We'd see about that.

In the seat next to me, Lexie shot me a disgruntled look. "I don't see why you want to get rid of it," she told me. "Maybe if you hadn't always had your Sight, maybe if your Sight took a really long time to come, you wouldn't be so ready to get rid of it." Lexie shot a tortured look at our mother.

"It will come, Lexie," my mom told her. My dad turned on the radio. The Sight wasn't one of his favorite topics of conversation, especially lately.

According to my mom, all the women in her family were gifted with some version of the Sight, an ability to see what others could not. My mom's gift had a lot to do with her überradar. She saw things as they happened, whether she was there watching or not. When I'd gotten lost as a child, she'd always known where to find me. Mom's Sight was particularly useful for finding the lost.

My Sight wasn't particularly useful for anything

except confirming my freak-of-nature status (not that it needed to be confirmed after the Face on Window Incident . . . just ask the girls in the convertible).

For as long as I could remember, I'd seen the world differently from other kids. Every person I met, every person I even so much as saw on television or in a movie, was surrounded by a small moving quantity of colored light. My mom called them auras. As a child, I'd called them colors.

Now, I mostly called them unwanted. It was one thing around people I'd always known, to see their colors and to know what the colors meant, but meeting new people was exhausting, especially when, for instance, their auras stood perfectly and freakishly still as they stared me down from inside a perky blue convertible. I'd gotten along fine at my old high school, but I'd seen far too many Hollywood movies about the trials and tribulations of transferring in the middle of sophomore year to have a good feeling about this whole starting-a-new-high-school thing. Then again, I was from California. This was Oklahoma. That had to buy me something, right?

"I mean, come on. Ok-la-ho-ma," I muttered out loud. My mom glanced back at me curiously, and I immediately looked away from her and down at my hand. Today I was green, which honestly made very little sense. In my experience, most people had a single base color that indicated certain things about their personality, and though the shade varied from moment to moment, the light always moving and glowing differently, the base color did not.

My mom was a green, which meant she had nurturing as a primary characteristic. The tone of the color changed depending on her mood, the brightness depending on her actions. I could see the same types of changes for everyone else. When I was little, I'd always known when people had done something truly horrible, because their colors became dim and washed out, an awful color that made me shudder, a color so terrible that it didn't have a name. I'd always called it Garn. Somehow, it had seemed logical when I was four and trying to explain the exact shade to my mom.

My dad was a no-nonsense golden brown.

Lexie was a cheerful pink.

My colors never knew how to stay put. When I looked at my own hands, I saw every color, and depending on the day, one color or another pulled to the forefront of my lights.

I closed my eyes. As long as they were closed, I didn't have to wonder why today was a green day for me, and as long as I pretended to sleep, I didn't have to worry about my mom asking any questions about Paul.

Beside me, Lexie was still grumbling. "Some people take the Sight for granted," she said, and without opening my eyes and without even a smudge of my mom's gift for seeing things that my eyes did not, I knew that Lexie was glaring at me reproachfully. She was thirteen,

8

and she'd still shown no signs of any advanced Sight. Personally, I thought she was lucky. Lexie never had any problems fitting in anywhere. In fact, chances were quite good that within thirty minutes of settling into her room in our new house, she'd have five new best friends, all of whom thought she was the greatest person to ever walk this earth, and she'd have at least four potential love interests identified and well on their way to worshipping her.

In my vaunted opinion, the way Lexie attracted people was a far better gift than any kind of supernatural vision. Lexie, of course, did not agree. The grass was always greener and whatnot. I tried not to think about the fact that at the moment, I was greener too.

"Can we please change the subject?" my father asked from the front seat, his voice tense. I wondered what he was so grumpy about. It had been his decision to leave home in the first place, his and my mom's. It wasn't like I was dragging him halfway across the country away from all of his friends and quite possibly the love of his life.

You're not being fair, my tiny inner voice told me.

Shut up, I told the voice.

You shut up, the voice said back.

I groaned out loud. A conscience was such an inconvenient thing to have.

Other consciences let their masters have PMS-y moments, I complained silently. Then I sighed. In the great battle of Lissy James vs. the annoying inner voice, the annoying inner voice was winning, because deep down, I knew that my parents hadn't really wanted to move either. I was old enough that I knew why we were moving, why we had to move.

A little boy was dead, the murderer still at large, and the only reason they'd found the body at all was my mother. She'd seen his death in her mind's eye, so she'd known where to tell the police to find the body. To people who didn't believe in the Sight, that was incriminating. She'd helped the police out on dozens of cases, returned dozens of missing children home, and they'd simply looked the other way and been grateful for her freely given help. But this one failure had changed everything.

If I was being honest with myself, we hadn't had much of a choice about leaving, not really. It wasn't safe for my mom in town anymore. The same people who had adored her when she'd been a hero hated her now. The colors of our entire coastal town had changed after four-year-old Cody Park's body had been found under an old dock, burned almost beyond recognition, exactly as my mom had seen it.

All the colors were now a little bit dimmer, my mom's included. Even as I argued with my conscience, her green lights were pulled tight to her face, the color muted and the movement restrained. The failure was killing her inside. As we drove, for a moment her aura expanded and darkened to a green so dark it was almost black, and I knew she was having a reflash, seeing Cody's body again and knowing she could do nothing about it.

It was no wonder my dad didn't want to talk about the Sight. I didn't particularly want to talk about it either. For all I cared, the Sight could go straight to Hades. I was sick of it all.

So there I was, stuck in the backseat of my parents' car, looking out the window and wondering why in the world life took the turns it did. I knew exactly what we'd left behind. Paradise. And for what? Some fast-food-induced dreams, a numb face, and Oklahoma, a state whose contents, as far as I could tell, consisted entirely of a bunch of grass and three long-haired girls who were Olympic-level snarlers. For all I knew, the snarlers were Oklahoma's claim to fame. As far as my friends from home and I had always been concerned, Oklahoma was the state where all the people had two first names and danced at hoedowns.

I decided right then and there that there would be no hoeing of the down for me. None whatsoever. Not even if that was what Mary Sue, Anna Beth, Berta Joy (I'd already named the snarlers), and the other four teenagers in this state insisted was all the rage.

My mom chuckled at the expression on my face, and I figured that my firm-decision look was probably one of those expressions that wasn't exactly flattering.

"You really should practice those looks in the mirror," Lexie told me earnestly. I tried to glare at her, but I couldn't. Her pink was too bright and her voice too eager-to-please for me to do anything but smile at her. Darn those colors.

"Almost there," my mom said, like that was something to be excited about. "Look, there's the library."

She sounded like such a little kid that I almost expected her to add "That's where the books live."

Cut her some slack, my inner voice said. *At least her colors are back to their normal shade. Would you rather she was still caught up in the reflash?*

I couldn't think of a good enough response, and round two of Lissy vs. the inner voice also went to the voice.

Beside me, Lexie stared out the window, a contemplative look on her pixie face. She had a small mouth and a tiny nose that fit daintily into place, with big blue eyes that were way too innocent-looking for her own good. Her hair was strawberry blond and perfectly straight.

My hair was a medium brown shade, my eyes the same color, and my features neither delicate nor sharp. My cheekbones were almost invisible. Lexie and I didn't look much alike, and I wasn't sure which one of us had gotten the better end of the deal. No matter how old she got, Lexie would always look younger than she was, and no matter how old I got, my forehead would always be too long. For now, it was a toss-up. Lexie's contemplative look suited her, and I had a feeling that had something to do with the fact that there was a 97 percent chance she'd been practicing it in front of a mirror.

"What are you thinking about, Lex?" I asked her softly, curbing another yawn.

Lexie continued staring out the window as she answered me. "Oklahoma and school." With my little sister, what you saw was what you got. She wasn't always the smoothest person in the world, but despite the mirror practicing, she was genuine, and she never lied. If Lexie said she was thinking about Oklahoma and school, then she was thinking about Oklahoma and school. The closest she could come to a lie was omitting some tasty tidbit of information that she didn't want broadcast.

Even though she hadn't said it out loud, I knew from the look on her face that Lexie was also thinking about the Sight. These days, it seemed to be on her mind more and more. When would she understand that she was the lucky one and stop wishing for the day when her power would come?

I so wasn't up to arguing with her about it. The bright pink aura was awfully hard to argue with, and honestly, I had the distinct feeling that I was going to need to save up all my energy for the next few days: a new town, a new school, and a promise to myself to be normal, no matter what my mom said. The silent promise had barely crossed my mind when we pulled around a corner just in time to see a woman bend down and put a leash on some kind of small, fuzzy animal.

She smiled and waved. The dog (or possibly the furry rat) yipped in excitement.

"People are just friendlier in this part of the country," my dad said, amazed.

I opened my mouth, but words didn't come out. Even through the car window, I could see the woman's aura: red with the smallest streak of a nameless color that made my stomach roll and sent a chill down my spine.

Garn.

Despite her friendly wave and cute little rat dog, this woman wasn't the kind of person we wanted to be friends with. She had to have done something awful to have her lights tinged with the color of nothingness, even as small as the streak was.

Shadows and light. Shadows and colors and light.

Images from my dream jumped into my head, and I shuddered as I tore my eyes away from the woman's aura just in time to catch a glimpse of the blue convertible parked next door.

"This is it." I swallowed hard at my dad's words as we pulled into a driveway suspiciously close to the convertible. Garn and snarling girls in one neighborhood. It gave me a headache even thinking about it.

Welcome to Oklahoma, Lissy James, I thought, *whether you like it or not.*

2

purple

Lexie was the first one out of the car, and I was the last. Stepping into the sunlight after having been in the car since obscenely early that morning, I blinked and rubbed the corners of my eyes. Was it always this bright in Oklahoma? Still a little fazed by the extra-strength sunlight, I turned toward the sound of my mom's voice.

"Isn't the house beautiful?" As the words left her mouth, her aura shuddered almost imperceptibly, and its color shifted. All of a sudden, I felt like I was looking at her colors through sunglasses. I narrowed my eyes at her, wondering if she'd had a sudden mood change, but "isn't it beautiful" didn't exactly scream of sudden depression.

I shrugged. Maybe in Oklahoma the super-size sun was so bright that everything else seemed just a little bit duller in comparison. Besides, I had more important things to deal with, non-aura-related things that didn't mess with Project Normal, like hoping that there was

15

more than one tiny blue convertible in the state of Oklahoma and trying to find a way to tell my mom what I thought of our new house without deeply insulting her.

"It's . . ." I trailed off. There were no words.

"It's big," Lexie finished for me. "And old." She paused for a moment and then smiled again. "It looks like it would be haunted, but it's not."

"Are you sure about that?" I asked her, wiggling my eyebrows at her in a manner specifically designed to freak her out.

"Yes, I'm sure," she said firmly, "and you really should practice that look in the mirror, Lissy, because you just look bizarre. You don't want people to think you're a freak." There was no malice whatsoever in Lexie's voice. She was completely serious.

"I *am* a freak," I said under my breath. My mom cast a sideways look in my general direction, and then very deliberately ignored me. She moved forward, reached for the doorknob, and twisted it. As the door swung open, I arched an eyebrow at my dad. Hadn't anyone thought to lock the door?

"People don't always lock their doors here," my dad replied, expertly reading my facial expression. "It's a small community."

"Not as small as everyone thinks," Lexie chirped. She didn't pause a moment before she changed topics. "Do you think there are any boys my age around here?"

If there were, I was willing to bet they'd be eating out of her hand in a week.

16

As I stepped onto the front porch of the old house that my delusional parents expected me to call home, I heard my mom's squeal from inside, followed by a booming male voice. "Katie!"

"Corey!" As soon as my uncle's name was out of my mom's mouth, Lexie and I looked at each other and bolted into the house. Both of us were big fans of Uncle Corey.

I wondered if I was old enough yet to just call him by his first name. Saying "Uncle Corey" made me feel like I was about nine years old.

"How are my girls?" he asked, pulling us both into a big bear hug.

"Just peachy," I replied. Uncle Corey grinned, and I took a step back and looked at him, really looked at him. The light around his body was a soft golden yellow, less brown than my dad, but not the neon tennis ball yellow I saw on a lot of show-offy teenage guys. Its movement was controlled, and his aura was larger than most I'd seen, extending well past the tips of his fingers and the top of his head.

"You look good," I told him. The tone of his lights looked . . . happy.

He simply cocked one eyebrow at me. "Do I now?" he asked, his voice mild. As a male in my mother's family, he'd grown up hearing about the Sight, but didn't have his own gift. That was one of the reasons that Lexie liked him so much, and honestly, I didn't mind his skepticism. It was refreshing. I didn't want to be gifted, as my mother

17

so eloquently put it, because gifted translated directly to special, special to different, and different to relegated to sitting at the freak table at lunch.

In Uncle Corey's mind, I was exactly the same as every other teenager, and I loved him for that, too.

A flash of silver light had me looking out the window, and I groaned. I'd only ever met one person in my life with a silver aura. My grandmother. Walking over to the window, I saw her approaching the house on foot, carrying what looked like a paper bag.

From here, I couldn't tell what exactly she was wearing, only that it was a particularly hideous shade of orange and that there was a distinct chance that it was a muumuu. An orange muumuu didn't exactly fit in with my mental image of what a sweet old woman with two children and two grandchildren should be wearing, especially when one of those grandchildren was me.

"Come!"

I rolled my eyes but started toward the porch as my grandmother made her way up the walkway. Grams never minced words when it came to summoning us. She just yelled out whatever single-word command came to mind, and whoever she was yelling at automatically did whatever they were told. It was very annoying, especially when I was the person coming because of her barked order.

Lexie joined me on the porch. "Grams is here," she announced needlessly. Her pink light had pulled closer to her skin, and though I didn't know exactly what it

18

meant, I felt like she could probably use a hug. She looked up at me, her eyes a little sad.

"Do you think Grams knows?" Lexie asked me in a whisper when Grams was still half a yard away.

"Knows what?" I asked.

Lexie shrugged and then met my eyes. "You know," she said. "Do you think she knows that I still haven't gotten my Sight?"

So that was what the puppy dog eyes were about. I didn't answer Lexie. I wanted to smack her. For a second there, I'd thought she was actually upset about moving, but really she was just nervous about seeing our grandmother and telling her that she was still Blind.

"There are my beautiful grandchildren," my grandmother said, her voice so loud and booming that the movers carrying boxes into the house stopped to stare at her.

"Continue!" she yelled. The movers immediately went back to work.

"Hi, Grams," Lexie said, running the last few steps to give our grandmother a hug. Grams stared at Lexie for a moment, her forehead wrinkled in thought, and then she squeezed her so tightly I thought Lexie was going to pop.

"Growing up, are you, my fairy girl?" she asked. Lexie didn't say anything, but she didn't look embarrassed at the term of endearment either. Then again, "fairy girl" was a step up from "Weasel."

"And what about you, Lissy of the Morning?" she

asked me. I had no idea where she was pulling the nick-names from, though had I been either more vulgar or a little bit braver, I would have ventured a guess.

I hugged her, wondering why she smelled like cinna-mon, garlic, and dirt all at the same time.

"How do I look?" she asked me immediately after she released me from her death grip hug.

Ignoring the fact that the hideous orange garment was in fact a muumuu, I looked at her for a moment. The sil-ver color clung to her body, shining but dull in compari-son to the glaring sunlight. "Still silver," I told her.

She waited. "That's it?" she asked. "What about breadth?" I stared at her blankly. "Tension? Motion? What about brightness, contrast, and tonal quality?"

"Ummm . . . it looks kind of like you're standing in the shade," I told her, chewing on the inside of my cheek. *Or like I'm wearing sunglasses,* I thought.

"I *am* standing in the shade," Grams repeated, her hands on her hips. She sighed a very aggrieved sigh and turned to my mom. "Haven't you taught her anything, Kathryn?" I tried not to grin at my mom's obvious dis-comfort. She was only Kathryn with Grams when she was in trouble.

"What's there to learn?" I asked, coming to my mom's rescue even though I knew that I probably shouldn't risk opening my big mouth. "There are colors, big deal. I don't really care about that anymore, Grams." I could feel myself rambling on, and I could see that Grams was getting progressively unhappier with every word I said. I was quite simply digging myself a hole to be buried in, but I couldn't stop. "It's no big deal, Grams."

She huffed. "No big deal?" she asked, her voice at normal volume level. "It most certainly is a big deal. I cannot believe your mother has not seen to it that you girls are better trained." Grams cast a tortured look at my mom.

"Don't be ridiculous, Mother," Uncle Corey broke in. "Katie's been busy, and the girls have school and their friends and activities. They don't have time for your superstitious nonsense."

Grams completely ignored him. She and Corey had been having this debate for years. He was a doctor with a scientific mind, and nothing either she or my mother had said or done had been able to convince him that the Sight actually existed. He had explained it all to me once, in terms of family legends and psychological phenomena. Even thinking the words "psychological phenomena" made me feel a lot smarter than I really was. I made a mental note to throw them into casual conversation sometime.

"The girls will study with me," Grams proclaimed. I looked at my mom, alarmed. Surely she wouldn't just hand us over to Grams for some voodoo lesson when she knew how much I didn't want to think about my so-called gift. She also knew that it would kill Lexie if she had to face the fact that she didn't yet have her part in the legacy every single day. My mother was a smart woman. She would figure a way around all this.

"I think that's a wonderful idea, Mother," my mom said. "Not every day, of course, because the girls start school tomorrow, but a couple of lessons a week might be just the ticket."

I stared at my mom as if she had suddenly sprouted antlers. It occurred to me that I would have preferred it if she'd suddenly sprouted antlers. At least that way, I could have hung a coat on her or something, but as it was, she wasn't doing me much good at all.

"Excellent," my grandmother said. The sound of footsteps made Grams turn around. "Guests!" she boomed.

Without warning, our lawn had been taken over by a flock of impeccably groomed, perfect-bodied teenagers. Upon closer inspection, I discovered that the one on the left, surrounded by a pastel green aura, was older than she looked, probably thirty or thirty-five. The others were younger, near my age, and I didn't have to look at their auras to know that I'd seen them before.

The snarlers had arrived. I could only hope that they (a) hadn't seen up my nose, and (b) didn't recognize me without my face smushed up against a glass surface. I tried not to stare at them, but I couldn't help it. They were tanned and highlighted and plucked to perfection. Had I not seen their auras, I probably would have thought they were soulless fembots or something. I couldn't keep my eyes from focusing in on their auras, and when I looked at them, *really* looked at them, I almost immediately wished that I hadn't.

Two of them were purple. Not lavender, not violet.

Purple. I hated purples. I'd never met a single purple person that I'd liked. Purples were catty and territorial, and for the most part they all seemed to think I made a more-than-suitable scratching post. One of the purple girls smiled at me, and her dreadful purple lights stood perfectly still.

I smiled tentatively back at her. If she wanted to be friendly to the new kid, I wasn't about to throw it back in her face, even if the purple light surrounding her made me want to puke.

"Emily, Lilah," Uncle Corey said, stepping in to take charge, "this is my sister, Katie, her husband, Patrick, and their daughters, Lissy and Lexie."

He'd forgotten to introduce me as Felicity. If I couldn't count on Uncle Corey for that, I couldn't really count on anyone supporting Project Name Change.

He turned back to our family. "This is Emily Covington and her daughter, Lilah." The dark-haired, eyebrow-arching purple. "Emily and I work together at the hospital. Lilah's a junior at the high school." I'd never heard Uncle Corey's voice sound so stiff and formal.

For a moment, Lilah and I stared at each other, and then, without saying hello, she inclined her head slightly toward the other two girls. The purple on the left, the fake blonde, was about to fall out of her tiny white tank top. She smiled at me, but as she did, her aura pulled tight to her face, making the smile look as fake as her breasts did. "This is Tracy." Lilah paused for just a moment longer, and I saw the last member of their little trio narrow her eyes

23

almost imperceptibly at Lilah. In fact, if I hadn't noticed the way the girl's fuchsia colors buzzed with annoyance, I might not have picked up on it at all.

Ugggg, I thought in anticipation. There were some colors that should just never be aura colors. Fuchsia was one of them.

"And Fuchsia."

It took me a minute after Lilah finally introduced the last girl to figure out that Fuchsia was actually her name. I opened my mouth to say something, but I was dumbstruck. Fuchsia? Fuchsia?! Who named their kid Fuchsia?

"Hi," Lexie said brightly, always the first one to recover her voice. "I'm going to be an eighth grader, so we won't be in school together, but if you know anything about the eighth grade that you'd like to share, I'm all ears."

The older woman, Emily, smiled at Lexie, won over by the way she easily chatted up complete strangers. Even Lilah, who looked far too old to be Emily's daughter, shot a smirk that might have been part-smile in Lexie's general direction. Fuchsia looked down at her nails. Tracy, her aura still pulled tight to her face, dismissed Lexie without so much as another fake smile.

After a long, awkward pause, I felt my mom eyeballing me, so I introduced myself.

"I'm Felicity," I said, finding the name awkward on my lips after all these years of having my given name shortened to Lissy. "I'll be a sophomore this year."

Lilah gave me a look that clearly said "Like I care." I could practically feel myself blushing. Lilah was a purple, all right. Anyone who could make me feel this stupid just for introducing myself had to be a purple.

"Why don't you girls show Lexie and Lissy around the neighborhood?" Emily said to her daughter, trading looks with my uncle. Her green aura expanded toward his, touching it softly, and my uncle's golden lights moved in sync with hers. I averted my eyes. I so wasn't in the mood to watch my uncle aura-flirt, especially with purple Lilah's mother.

Lilah sent Lexie and me a too-bright smile that all three of us knew was for the adults' benefit. "Oh. We were just heading out to Fuchsia's house." Lilah shrugged, giving us a sheepish look that I totally would have bought if the light surrounding her body hadn't picked that moment to turn so dark a purple that it was almost black. "Maybe another time." Lilah paused and looked me up and down. "Or you could come if you want to," she offered after what seemed like an eternity. She sounded absolutely thrilled about the prospect.

Fuchsia frowned at Lilah, but recovered quickly. "Yes," she said, her voice high and perky. "Come."

"It'll be fun," Tracy chimed in.

Oh God. Coming from her, it sounded more like "I'll get you, my pretty" than an invitation to hang out with them.

"Go on, Lissy," my mom said. "Unpacking can wait."

Thanks, Mom, I said silently, as I glanced back at the girls. *Thanks a lot.*

"Lexie?" Surprisingly, my voice sounded perfectly

25

calm. I'd like to say that I asked my sister to come along out of good, older-sisterly feelings, but I totally just wanted something, anything, to keep me from being alone with the snarlers.

"I think I'm going to hang out here," Lexie said. "There's got to be some people my age around here somewhere, and I bet Emily and Uncle Corey can help me find some phone numbers or something."

I correctly interpreted "people" as "boys." Traitor.

Lilah stood on the lawn waiting for me, and as I took a step toward her, golden and pale green lights flashed in the corner of my eye. Despite my better judgment, I turned back to look at Emily and Uncle Corey. His aura was jutting out at points, tiny spindles of yellow light pushing out from his body. I shook my head and blinked, and the next moment, everything was back to normal.

"Are you coming or aren't you?" Lilah's voice cut through the air, and I shuddered. Purple. My uncle's lights were all over her mom's, and she just had to be a purple.

"I'm coming," I said.

Lilah nodded, and then, without another word, she flounced off across the street, Fuchsia and Tracy at her heels. Biting my bottom lip, I followed.

Why did I totally feel like I was about to walk the plank?

3

fuchsia

I might have enjoyed the ride in Fuchsia's convertible if it hadn't been for the company. Three awful auras in one tiny car? So not my idea of a good time.

"I can't even believe she did that. I mean, who does she think she is? Like anyone can just go to the mall and buy those shoes."

As Tracy continued her tirade, I half expected her to add "And for that she must die." Instead, she just shook her head. "She's totally copying you, Lilah. It's pathetic when you really think about it."

From the shotgun seat, Lilah turned around and glared at Tracy. "Then don't." Apparently, Lilah wasn't enjoying Tracy blabbing on and on about some sophomore who'd had the gall to go to the mall and buy shoes any more than I was. Beside me, I could practically feel Tracy's purple lights quiver at the tone of Lilah's voice, but by the time I turned to look at her, her aura was standing perfectly still, and she was smiling in my direction.

Uh-oh.

"So is *that* what people are wearing in California?"

I looked down at my T-shirt and jeans. They were wrinkled, too big, and, in a car full of fembots, totally out of place. What did they expect? I'd been riding in a car for two and a half days. Then again, Tracy had brought up California, not me. Maybe she wasn't being sarcastic. I mean, this was Oklahoma. Maybe if I told them this *was* what people were wearing in California, that Natalie Portman had a pair of jeans just like these, they'd just smile and nod. I was the big-city girl, come to bring fashion to the poor, deprived people of Oklahoma.

"More or less," I said, shrugging off the disbelieving look Tracy gave me.

"You can't expect everyone from California to care about the way they look," Fuchsia said as she flipped on the turn signal. So much for me bringing fashion to the poor, deprived people of Oklahoma. "I mean, think about it. The average person in California probably isn't any prettier than the average person anywhere else, but since they've got Hollywood there, they're a lot uglier in comparison than they would be anywhere else, you know?"

I honestly tried to figure out what she was saying. Fuchsia logic was a horrible thing to try to follow.

"If you know you'll never be a J.Lo or a Reese, why bother?" Fuchsia said. "Right, Lissy?" Fuchsia's voice dripped with sugary sweetness.

"Right," I found myself saying before I had even halfway worked out what I was supposed to be saying "right" to.

"No offense or anything, but you might want to try to 'bother' a little more here," Lilah said casually. I craned my neck, trying to see what her aura was up to, but from the backseat, all I could see was the back of her ponytail, dark hair tinted with purple light. Was Lilah trying to give me advice or a warning?

Or was it both?

"I like your car." I wasn't exactly the master of the subject change, but I had to say something, and talking about California so wasn't going the way I'd hoped it would.

"Oh, this?" Fuchsia asked flippantly. "It's not as nice as my old one, but Daddy got all pissy when I wrecked the other one."

"Other *ones*," Lilah reminded her.

Fuchsia shrugged. "Whatever. You can't drive yet, can you, Lissy?"

"No." One-word answers seemed safe. "I'll be sixteen in another couple of months."

"It's funny," Fuchsia said with a charming little giggle. "You seem younger."

I should have stuck to the one-word answer.

"So I was talking to Jackson Hare the other day." Lilah abruptly changed the subject.

"What did he say?" Even the idea of this Jackson Hare person had Fuchsia's aura bouncing back and forth at warp speed. I was practically getting motion sickness.

"Oh, you know. A little of this. A little of that."

Fuchsia pulled into a driveway on our left, and then turned to look at Lilah, but before she could say so much as a word, Lilah was out of the car. "Shall we?" she asked, and I could tell from the way Fuchsia's aura stopped moving that I wasn't the only one who sensed that Lilah had said all she was going to say about Jackson Hare.

Stepping out of the car to stand next to Lilah, I got a better look at the colored lights surrounding her body. To my surprise, they were lighter, almost lavender. I stared at her aura for a moment, and as I did, I felt my whole body going numb.

Three intertwining circles, rings of different colors on a silver shield.

I blinked hard once, twice, three times, and the images were gone.

"Do you have something in your eye?" Tracy's voice broke into my thoughts. I got the distinct feeling that hard blinking was one of those looks that Lexie would have told me to practice in the mirror.

"Yeah," I said, casting a sideways glance at Lilah. "I did."

Five minutes later, I discovered that there was definitely something worse than being in a car with two purples and a fuchsia named Fuchsia.

"So do you have a boyfriend?"

Being in a room with two purples and a fuchsia.

Paul. I couldn't keep his name from coming to my mind. Paul on the beach, saying goodbye. Paul collapsed on the couch next to me, laughing at horrible B-movies. Paul . . .

"Look at her. She's totally blushing."

"What's his name?"

"Is he from California?"

"What's he look like?"

"Have you guys done it?"

As they shot questions at me, their auras twisted and turned, melting into one another at the edges and expanding until the room was a mess of purple and pink, pink and purple, advancing on me by the second.

"He's not exactly my boyfriend." I glanced away from their probing eyes.

"Did he break up with you?"

"OMG, he totally cheated on you, didn't he?"

"You're a virgin, aren't you?" The last comment came from Lilah, and unlike the others, it was said in an almost bored tone. I turned my eyes on her, and she stared back at me for a moment. Her aura shrank, drooping, but the expression on her face never changed from a small, tight smile on pursed lips.

"He broke up with you because you wouldn't have sex with him," Fuchsia concluded. "That's terrible."

"Totally," Tracy agreed immediately. "But don't worry. We won't tell anyone."

So *that* was why Lilah's aura was doing the guilty drooping thing. She'd sentenced me to being the new girl who got dumped for being a prude. I wasn't even positive that she'd meant to (for that matter, I wasn't even fully convinced that *she* wasn't a virgin), and somehow, that made things even worse. Some people had to try to be bitchy.

31

Some people didn't.

The sound of a door opening blared from Fuchsia's computer, and the four of us turned to stare at the screen. Fuchsia fiddled with her mouse for a second and clicked on her buddy list.

"So who's signed on?" Tracy asked. "Anyone interesting?"

Translation: anyone important?

Fuchsia snorted. "Not hardly," she said. "I unblocked some of the Nons this week, because I totally needed to find someone to give me the answers to this take-home test, and now they're all IM-ing me all the time, like I honestly don't have something better to do than sit around and Non it up."

"Nons?" I asked. I tried casually to get a better look at the buddy list.

"Nons," Lilah repeated. "Nonfactors, nonplayers."

"Losers," Fuchsia clarified.

"Non-Goldens," all three girls said at once.

"Goldens?" I asked.

Fuchsia gestured toward her buddy list. "You'll learn quickly that at Emory High, there are two kinds of people: those that matter"—she pointed to one section of her buddy list, entitled "Goldens"—"and those that don't." These names were at the bottom of the list, and there seemed to be three or four times more of them than there were of the others. The Goldens.

"Of course, there are different levels of Goldens," Fuchsia said. She gestured to the bottom subsection under that portion of her buddy list. "Hot," she said. She scrolled up the page a little. "Hotter." She paused again. "Hottest."

I was going to go out on a limb and guess that the present company, myself excluded, was on the hottest list.

"Hey!" Tracy said suddenly. "How come I'm only hotter?"

Fuchsia shrugged. "You were only hot," she said, "but then you got the boob job, dyed your hair blond, and started dating Tate. I can't bump you up more than one level, though, just because we're friends." Fuchsia did her best to sound shocked. "That would hardly be fair to anyone else."

As she spoke, Fuchsia's aura began to spindle, stretching at the edges until tiny little aura strings extended off in many directions.

Oh my gosh, I thought. *It's like she really does have snakes for hair.*

The little snaky tendrils lashed out at Tracy, smacking her aura a couple of times. Tracy's aura shrank back next to her body, and in the next instant, the entirety of her purple lights lunged toward me.

I physically jumped back, earning sketched-out looks from all three of the so-called Goldens. A second later, I blinked, and their auras settled back into place: no tendrils, no lunging, no nothing.

"So what's *your* screen name?" Tracy asked darkly.

The others turned to me expectantly.

I so did not want to see where my name went on that list. I had a feeling that was exactly why Tracy had asked me for my screen name in the first place.

"LissyLou45," I mumbled. I had to spell it out for them, but a moment later, Fuchsia's fingers were flying across her keyboard. She hit Enter and immediately minimized her buddy list. "Added it," she said with a grin.

Added it where? I wondered.

"Oooooh, Brock's online, Li," Fuchsia said, swiftly and conspicuously changing the subject.

Lilah grinned. "Let me talk to him," she ordered.

Fuchsia only hesitated for a moment before she slid to the side and let Lilah on the computer.

"The boys are playing football over on Bunting Street," Lilah said.

That was all it took, and the next instant, Lilah signed off Fuchsia's screen name, and the four of us were headed for Bunting Street, or, more accurately, the four of us were headed for the boys.

• • •

As soon as she parked the car, Fuchsia and Tracy pulled out lipstick and began to reapply it. I wasn't even wearing Chapstick. Lilah, of course, looked perfect without it.

"We're going to go ahead," Lilah said. "Come on."

As I walked behind her, following orders, her sleek, dark ponytail mocked me with the fact that, despite the awful humidity, it wasn't the least bit frizzy.

My mousy brown hair, on the other hand, had become the hair equivalent of a frizzed powder puff.

"This is the school," she told me without bothering to turn around. "Everyone hangs out on the lawn before first period, so getting to school early is a must unless you want to completely fall off the radar." She flicked one hand to the left, and I followed the gesture with my eyes. "That's the Non side of the lawn. Enough said."

Finally, we stopped when we came to a lawn full of boys playing football without their shirts on. One of them in particular caught my eye. With his dark hair and midnight blue aura, he reminded me of Paul.

"That's Brock," Lilah said, fingering the ends of her hair, a small smile on her face. "Brock Phillips. He was an all-state football player as a freshman, he's on the student council, he's a senior, he's Golden, and . . ." She trailed off, looking directly into my eyes and pausing for an elongated moment. "He's mine."

I tore my eyes away from him. A midnight blue with a bright purple? Now, that was just wrong. Of all the colors I'd been, I'd never once been a true purple.

"Nice," I said, only half meaning it.

"Yes," Lilah said, waving to Brock and then smiling pointedly at me. "It is."

Well, isn't that special? I grumbled silently.

Thunk. I was snapped out of my mental grumbling by the merciless connection of a football with the side of my head. I heard fits of giggles from a few feet away and noticed that Fuchsia and Tracy, freshly made up, had caught up with us.

Dazed, I rubbed the side of my head, and all around me, auras moved in a flash of light, twisting and turning, pulling against their boundaries and spindling like Uncle Corey's and Fuchsia's had earlier. A moment later, without warning, everything went back to normal, and all the auras stood perfectly still.

"Sorry," a voice said sheepishly, bringing me back to the present and my football-induced headache. "My bad." I looked up at a blond-haired guy who looked about my age.

"It's all right," I said, taking in his golden aura. It was almost the exact same shade as my uncle's.

"I'm Tate," he said simply.

"Lissy," I said, sticking my hand out to shake his and then feeling like a complete and utter loser for doing so.

"I know," Tate said, smiling at me and shaking my hand. "Word travels fast around here. You're Caroline Nowly's granddaughter, right? We heard you were coming."

I smiled up at him and belatedly nodded. He was at least six foot two, much taller than I was. He was undeniably droolworthy in a blatantly not-Paul way, and I had *shaken* his hand. What was wrong with me?

I felt Tracy's glare before I saw it. Her aura snaked back and forth possessively, and the look on her face was absolute murder. What had I done? Lilah leaned in and whispered lightly in my ear.

"Tate," she said simply, "is Tracy's." Which, of course,

36

meant that I wasn't allowed to be hit in the head by Tate's football, and I certainly wasn't allowed to shake his hand. That involved touching him, and from the dangerous glint in her narrowed eyes, I was pretty sure that touching Tracy's boyfriend was far worse a sin than going to the mall and buying a pair of shoes that I wasn't cool enough to wear.

Tate bent down to pick up the football, and Lilah's midnight blue Brock came running over a moment later. "Hi," he said, looking first at Lilah and then at me. "You okay?"

"She's fine," Lilah said, in a tone that clearly said that she didn't have time to go into all the many things she already knew were wrong with me. What was with her? She'd actually been borderline decent a few times over the past hour, and now she was making Fuchsia look like an amateur.

Brock's eyes held mine for a second longer, his blue lights moving in gentle waves, before he turned his attention back to Lilah.

"Your mom up at the house?" Brock asked her. She nodded, her arms crossed over her chest. "With Corey?" Brock asked, continuing his line of questioning.

Lilah nodded again, and I realized that there was definitely something more than aura flirting going on between Lilah's mom and my uncle.

Oh goody. That almost made us related. How very keen.

"We don't want to interrupt your game," Lilah said sweetly, leaning in to give him a kiss so long that it made my mouth hang open. If Lexie had been there, she totally would have whipped out a pen and paper and started taking notes. Luckily, I was a bit more subtle.

Brock pulled away from the kiss slowly. Then he smiled at me, and again, he reminded me of Paul, the blue light flowing gently around his skin, touching it softly.

"It was nice to meet you," he said, looking straight at me.

"Yeah," Tate echoed, his gold lights perfectly still.

"You too," I whispered, well aware of the fact that Lilah was glaring at me.

The boys turned to walk away, and as soon as they were out of earshot, Lilah turned her attention back to me. "Like I said," she said, not even bothering to turn around and look at me face to face. "Brock's mine." She paused, reading my thoughts perfectly. "And I wouldn't get any ideas about Tate either," she added. "Tracy really doesn't like it when other girls get ideas about Tate."

My new life was shaping up just fine and dandy. I was going to be stuck studying who knows what with Grams; something weird was going on in the aura department with all the flashing and spindles; Lilah, the purple with too-perfect hair, already had it in for me; Tracy was three seconds away from hiring a hit man; and seeing Brock Phillips had only reminded me how much I really missed Paul.

As we walked over toward Tracy and Fuchsia, Lilah flashed me a very fake and somewhat sinister smile.

"Welcome to Emory High," she said.

Somehow, it sounded like a threat.

4

golden

Paul leaned forward, his lips only centimeters away from mine. I could feel his breath on my face, and my heart beat viciously against my rib cage. This was it.

"He's mine." At the sharp and sultry words, Paul pulled away. I turned around and was greeted by dark purple lights.

I turned back to Paul, confused. What was Lilah doing here?

I opened my mouth, but no words came out. Lilah glared at me, and without any warning, Brock was standing beside her. "And he's mine," Lilah continued. The next second, the room was filled with boys, and for as far as I could see, blue lights shined outward from their bodies. "And he's mine, and he's mine, and he's mine."

The earth rumbled beneath my feet and fire exploded all around us. Lilah and the many Brock/Pauls didn't seem to notice. The room darkened, and a shadow settled over the blue auras.

"Color! Breadth! Tone!" Grams materialized behind me and

39

barked out the words, one at a time, as she went into some kind of strange tap-dancing routine. As she moved, the shadow fell over her aura.

I turned back to look at Lilah. Her purple lights vibrated, as bright as ever.

I looked down at my hand. My lights were shining a pale blue, framing the image that was embossed on my palm: three intertwining circles, rings of different colors on a silver shield.

Shadows and light and color, and then there was nothing.

I rolled over in bed and groaned. If dreams were omens, I wasn't feeling too great about my chances for a decent first day of school.

"And *he's* mine, and *he's* mine, and *he's* mine . . . ," I mimicked under my breath. "And if he's not mine, he's Tracy's, but mostly, they're allllll mine." I rolled my eyes and kicked my covers violently off. After lying there for a second, I crawled out of bed and went to battle against the great frizz that was my hair. Thirty-two minutes later, the frizz was still winning.

"Kitchen!"

At the sound of the sharp order, I stuck my head out of the bathroom. "What's Grams doing here?" I hissed in the general direction of Lexie's room.

Coming into the hallway, Lexie shrugged. "Maybe she's here to give us a quick lesson," she said. "Do you think lessons with Grams will make my Sight come sooner?"

"Lexie—"

"Your hair's a little frizzy," she said, "and Mom said we're leaving in fifteen minutes."

"Kitchen!" Grams bellowed again, annoyed that no one had immediately heeded her first command.

Lexie and I looked at each other. "Coming," we yelled back. I smoothed my hair into a ponytail as I ran down the steps and tried to banish the image of Grams tap-dancing from my mind. What was it with this place and me having weird dreams?

"Good morning, my loves," Grams said serenely as we walked into the kitchen, like she hadn't been bellowing commands at us a moment before. "Are you ready?" Something in her voice made me wonder if she was talking about the first day of school or something else altogether.

"Lexie, my sprite," Grams said, "be a darling and run down the street and tell Lilah her ride leaves in ten minutes."

"What?" I asked humorlessly. We were giving Lilah a ride? Was nothing sacred? She was already invading my dreams; did Lilah "The Boy Is Mine" Covington really have to invade the safety of my car space as well?

The second Lexie was out of the room, Grams turned to me. "You're not being fair to her, you know," she said right off.

I stared at her incredulously. "What are you talking about?"

"Lilah," she said. "She's a good girl. You should give her more of a chance. Things haven't been easy for her."

"I didn't do anything to her," I said. "But she and her friends totally hate me already."

"You don't know that," Grams said, playing around with something on the counter. "They took you with them yesterday, didn't they?"

I snorted. "Yeah, and then Lilah pretty much drew the war lines when she introduced me to her boyfriend, and you should see the way her aura looks at me."

"She and Lexie seem to get along fine," my grandmother said.

"Lexie gets along fine with everyone," I grumbled.

Grams smiled then, a knowing smile that irritated me. She didn't *know* anything. Or did she? I'd never really stopped to wonder what her Sight was. I groaned inwardly. It was entirely possible that my crazy grandmother, muumuus and all, knew something that I didn't.

"Sit," she said simply. I immediately sat, half annoyed with myself for following her orders.

"Now close your eyes," Grams said, and I got the distinct feeling that the Lilah conversation was over.

I closed my eyes. "Why am I doing this?" I asked.

"It's your first lesson," Grams replied. "Things are changing. It has begun, and before you can see, you must learn to listen."

Great, I thought. In addition to being an eccentric old lady with no fashion sense, my grandmother was quickly turning cryptic.

"Listen to what?" I asked. "I don't hear anything."

"Exactly," she said. I opened my eyes. This was stupid.

"No matter what your gift is," Grams said in a lecturing voice, "you must learn to clear your mind before the Sight can fully take hold."

I looked at Grams, a serious expression on my face. I wanted to make her understand. "I don't want it to take hold of me," I said. "I don't want it, Grams."

"That's not a choice you can make, Felicity Shannon James," she said softly. Hearing my full name made me think of everything I'd ever been told about Shannon, the woman all women in my family were named after, the first Seer in our line. It was Grams' way of pulling on my sense of obligation to the family and to my gift. "Now close your eyes and listen."

I closed my eyes with no intention of listening to anything and with every intention of banishing Shannon and all things Sight-related from my mind. Instead, I thought about California, and everyone I'd left behind. I missed the beach. I'd always lived next to the ocean, and even though Oklahoma didn't seem too bad and I'd yet to see a single cow, I missed being able to walk out my back door and onto the sand.

Three intertwining circles, rings of different colors on a silver shield. The image came unbidden into my head, and my grandmother's voice broke gently into my thoughts.

"The Sight is a precious gift, child, and a great responsibility. For generations, the women of our family have guarded the legacy and used it for the greater good. Some see the future through premonition, others the past through retronition, and still others are Distance Seers."

I knew she was referring to my mom's gift.

"Some see into people's hearts, others into their souls," she continued. I wondered which of these referred to my so-called gift. If I'd seen Lilah's soul, then I wasn't very impressed. "But all see only what they want to see."

I opened my eyes, my thoughts of California and Paul drifting slowly away. "That's not true," I said. "I don't want to see anything."

"You don't want to see everything either," my grandmother said softly.

"Isn't that sort of obvious?" I asked, crossing my arms over my chest and leaning back in the chair.

"One would think so," Grams said, but somehow, I didn't feel like I'd won the argument at all. "I cannot believe that my Katie has not trained you girls to better appreciate your gifts." She sighed and stood up. "You'll see," she promised me. I didn't particularly like the sound of that.

"I'll see what?" I asked. She didn't answer, and I got the feeling that I didn't want to know.

Twenty-three minutes later, my mom dropped Lilah and me off at the high school, and I couldn't quite get Grams' promise out of my head. Lilah had yet to say a single word to me except for telling me that she liked my shirt while her lights did the aura equivalent of an eye roll. As she stepped out of the car, her black hair fell gracefully to her shoulders, and her hips swayed gently back and forth with each step she took. I half expected to hear some sort of glamorous theme music playing in the background.

Lilah paused for a moment, turned around, and looked me up and down once. "Be careful who you talk to," she instructed. "You don't want to be a freak by association." Her purple was several shades lighter today, almost, but not quite, into the tolerable range between violet and lavender. I peered at her closely.

"Are you trying to say something?" I asked her, waiting and trying to wade through the purple-y goodness to what she was actually trying to tell me.

"You'll never be a Golden if you don't learn who's who right away," Lilah told me. "Trust me."

"A Golden," I echoed. I still couldn't get over how easy it was for her to say the word and mean it. Every time it crossed her lips, her aura expanded, and I got a distinct vibe off her: *We are Golden, we are special, we are teen gods.*

Lilah nodded her head toward one side of the lawn, and I noticed a cluster of girls with broad auras in every shade of purple, pink, and teal imaginable. Goldens, Lilah had said. Even if I hadn't received a crash course in Emory Social Scene 101, I wouldn't have needed a translator anymore. The popular, the elite, the Goldens who were really purple. Hot, hotter, and hottest: Tracy and Fuchsia, Tate and Brock, and a cluster of suntanned teenagers with perfectly sculpted bodies and auras that stayed in constant motion, fighting with each other for space and the attention of the opposite sex.

"What makes you think I'd want to be a Golden?" I asked. The word felt funny on my lips. If I had called Paul and told him that was what the popular kids were called here, he'd have laughed at me. It sounded ridiculous.

I followed Lilah's deliberate gaze to the part of the yard filled with athletic guys, all talking loudly and clapping each other on the shoulders.

"Because," Lilah replied knowingly, answering my question, "everyone does."

I seethed. Who did this girl think she was? She stalked off then, without bothering to say goodbye. How very Lilah of her.

I stood there for a moment, looking at all the people, their colors flashing gently all over the lawn: blues and greens, purples and pinks, teal, yellow, tan, red, and orange.

"You don't belong here," a voice said cheerfully from behind me.

I turned to find myself staring straight into Tracy's face. She was smiling, her aura pulled so tightly to her body that I almost couldn't even see it. It was becoming easier to picture her as a fembot, especially given the fact that her T-shirt clung to her fake boobs in a way that definitely wasn't rated PG.

"Excuse me?" I said, trying to reconcile this girl with

the one who'd chatted me up the day before, commiserating over the "fact" that my boyfriend had dumped me for not wanting to give it up.

"You walk in here like you're so cute, and so *California*, but you don't even have a clue."

"You're right," I said before my brain could talk my mouth into not moving. "I don't have a clue what you're talking about."

Apparently, that was the wrong thing to say. Tracy looked me up and down, the vibration of the purple lights letting me know that I wasn't the only one who wished that I had never come to Oklahoma. What was with these girls? I wasn't completely freakish-looking. I didn't wear all black or little-kid clothing, so why had they decided that I was completely and utterly hopeless in the popularity department? Tracy had even said I was cute (sort of, anyway), so it obviously wasn't the way I looked. It couldn't have been the fact that I'd shaken her boyfriend's hand. That was ridiculous.

Wasn't it?

"I know you're really sad because you broke up with your own boyfriend and everything, but I just thought you should know that everyone thinks it's really pathetic that you're so desperate."

I sent a steely glance Lilah's way and wondered if she had anything to do with the fact that Tracy had decided I was gunning for Tate. I mean, come on, it's not as if shaking his hand made me a seductress.

"Tracy, I didn't even have a boyfriend, and I'm not—"

"Whatever," the girl muttered, glaring at me before she turned, tossed her hair over her shoulder, and flounced away.

Everyone here was so very friendly.

"Don't mind her," a voice said softly from beside me. "That's Tracy Hillard. She thinks she's really something else. They all do, all of the Goldens."

"Goldens," I repeated dully. Tracy Hillard was definitely not golden in any way that I could see.

"The popular kids," the girl replied, a twinge of humor in her voice. "They think they run the school." The girl smiled just a bit.

"But they're wrong?" I asked, liking this girl already.

"You could say that," the girl replied, her voice level. "Or you could just say that they aren't the sharpest tools in the shed."

"And Lilah?" I asked, overcome with curiosity about what this girl would have to say about my new bestest friend and almost cousin.

"She's their leader," she said simply. "Tracy would like to be, and Fuchsia Reynolds would kill for it, but Lilah . . ." The girl shrugged. "Lilah's evil incarnate, and there's just no competing with that."

I paused for just a moment upon hearing that. Sure, Lilah had been less than friendly since she'd introduced me to Brock, and sure, even standing in the same room as her made me feel like some kind of antisocial amoeba, but evil incarnate? There were times when her aura was bearable, times when I almost felt like she was trying, in her own special Lilah way, to help me out.

I glanced back over at the Golden portion of the lawn. Lilah ran her hand down the back of Brock's neck.

Evil incarnate. I was willing to accept that.

"What about the guys?" I asked.

The girl grinned. "Some of them are jerks," she said. "Some of them aren't, but as Golden boys always date Golden girls, I have to say that they're not the brightest bunch in the world."

"I'm Lissy," I said, forgetting for the umpteenth time to introduce myself by my full name.

"Audra," the girl replied simply. She stuck her hand out to shake mine. I liked this girl already. From across the lawn, Lilah shook her head discreetly at me, and I got the message loud and clear: Audra was one of the freaks the purple princess had warned me about. Why was she bothering to warn me in the first place? It wasn't like she actually wanted me to be popular, was it?

Evil incarnate, I reminded myself.

"Come on," Audra said easily, gesturing to the side of the lawn opposite Lilah and her friends.

I hesitated for a minute. Audra didn't look freakish to me. Then again, I didn't look freakish to me either. Lilah, like most popular girls, saw the world through freak-tinted glasses, except when it came to looking at herself. Then, all of a sudden, the special glasses came off, and

49

she saw herself as perfection—the princess of the world, sans even the slightest hint of freak.

Out of the corner of my eye, I could see colors flashing on the Golden half of the lawn: blue, yellow, pink, and quite a bit of sparkling purple. I thought of what it had been like yesterday in Fuchsia's car. In Fuchsia's room. On the soccer field. The Golden auras danced as the girls laughed and smiled and flirted, waiting for new meat that they could swallow whole.

"Okay," I said bravely, turning my attention back to Audra. "Let's go."

I followed Audra, trying to avoid looking at the other kids too much. So many new auras were giving me a headache. Audra plopped down on the lawn, and as I pushed my colored Sight down in my mind, I tripped and fell, dropping my backpack and making a lovely crashing sound.

Great, I thought, *why not just hire a herald to blow some trumpets and make a "Hear ye, hear ye, here cometh the great freak" announcement?*

Grabbing my backpack in a humiliation-fueled death grip and picking myself up off the ground, I wondered if anyone had noticed. There was always hope that the herald had not been heard. I looked around. Everyone was staring at me.

Tracy leaned over to whisper something in Fuchsia's ear, and their colored lights vibrated as they laughed riotously over whatever Tracy had said.

My gut instinct, being as incredibly developed as it was, told me that they had indeed noticed. Not wanting to draw any more attention to myself, I sat down next to Audra.

"Graceful," she commented wryly, but there was nothing mean in her voice. Her aura expanded for a moment and then contracted again in a quick motion I associated with sarcasm. I tilted my head and considered her color: peach with not even the least hint of true orange.

She was still giving me that good-natured sarcastic stare, so I struggled to grin back. I'd never been very good at laughing at myself. "I try," I said in reply to her comment. In case she didn't pick up on my meaning, I elaborated. "To be graceful," I said awkwardly. "I try."

Audra looked across the lawn, very kindly changing the subject. I followed her gaze to see Lilah standing next to her oh-so-muscle-y boyfriend.

"Your cousin doesn't like me very much," Audra told me.

"She's not my cousin," I replied. "And why doesn't Lilah like you?"

"She might as well be your cousin," Audra stated matter-of-factly. "Your uncle and her mom are the town's hottest couple these days. As for why she doesn't like me, who knows why any of the Goldens dislike some of us Nons more than others."

"Nons?" I asked, wrinkling my nose in what I was sure was an unflattering manner. I made a silent pact with myself to start practicing my faces in the mirror and an equally silent promise that I'd die before I let Lexie realize I was taking her advice.

"Non-Goldens," Audra replied. "Nons."

"I know what it means," I said. "It just seems . . . you know . . . kind of weird that . . ."

"That we say it too?" Audra asked.

I nodded.

Audra shrugged. "You get used to it after a while."

I didn't say anything out loud, but the fact that they had specific names for the popular and unpopular crowds kind of freaked me out. At my old school, everyone had known who the really popular kids were, but it hadn't been so set in stone, and there had been marginally popular kids. I had always liked to count myself among them, even if I was sort of in the bottom rung of those not-popular-not-unpopular types.

I glanced around. Were things really so different here? The colors all over the yard moved as all the kids interacted with each other. The motion was more than just a little bit distracting, especially since I wasn't very familiar with any of these auras and none of them were standing still. Like Audra's, some were expanding, others were contracting or rippling in waves of light, and all the auras moved as their owners walked or shifted positions. The result was becoming more than I could reasonably handle, especially since the last thing I wanted was a repeat of the Herald of Freakdom incident.

"Are you all right?" Audra asked me.

I nodded and took a deep breath, closing my eyes for a moment to relax. I had a feeling that this was going to be a very, very long day, especially if Tracy didn't stop glaring at me. Pushing the thought out of my mind, I took a deep breath, preparing myself to open my eyes again and allowing myself one moment of peacefulness before the bombardment of the strobe light aura fest began again.

When I finally opened my eyes, I gasped, and the power of what I saw threw my body back against the ground, hard.

If I'd thought it looked bad before, it was a million times worse now. All around me and all around the yard, I saw streams of light, some no bigger than strings, some the thickness of a jump rope. They were all different colors, and they extended from every single person in sight in every shade imaginable.

Forcing myself to concentrate, I turned to look at Audra. Her peach aura was still firmly attached to her body, staying relatively motionless, but at points it extended out in tiny spindles. Concentrating on deciphering the web of peach-tinted strings, I followed one. It stuck out from her shoulder and floated easily in the air for about three feet away from her body, where it connected with a blue string. I followed the blue string back to its owner and arrived at my own body.

This was definitely more than a little weird.

"Are you okay?" Audra asked me again.

I still didn't say anything. Instead, I stared at her,

following the rest of her strings. She was connected to a guy about our age who was pale to the nth degree and a middle-aged man walking briskly toward the building. Several streams of light ran off in various directions, too long for me to see quite where they were going or who they connected her to.

"Lissy, are you okay?" Audra asked a little louder, completely sketched out. Several of the Goldens looked over in our direction, their light strings becoming tauter as they did.

I nodded finally. "Yeah," I said, looking around the schoolyard at the thousands of tiny beams of light that connected the people standing there to each other. "I'm okay."

Just then a bell sounded, and everyone began to file into the building.

"That's the warning bell," Audra said. "Class starts in five minutes. We'd better get going. What class do you have first?" I could tell that she was making a real effort to change the subject from my state of okay-ness, like she didn't want me to feel too awkward. I appreciated it, and wondered what in the world was wrong with Lilah that she would have warned me against Audra.

"History," I replied, tearing my eyes away from the tangled lights all around me and looking down at my schedule. My uncle had picked it up for me, and I had spent a good hour the night before looking at it and trying to get a nice, temporary dose of premonition as to what it might indicate about the year to come. Unfortunately, I didn't have premonition, and the Sight wasn't the kind of thing that came in spurts, present weird Aura Vision changes excluded.

Audra grinned. "History," she commented wryly. "Good luck. Maybe I'll see you at lunch." Audra took off toward the building, and before I could so much as reply, she was gone and I was alone in the middle of the big, bad high school lawn.

I took a deep breath and started to walk toward the building, pausing every few steps because walking through the massive tangle of aura strings was starting to freak me out. Every time I stepped forward, I saw a bunch of them blocking my path, and since everyone else was moving too, I felt like I was being wrapped up in a bunch of neon threads.

"What are you doing?" a voice hissed in my ear. "Do you *want* everyone to think that you're a total loser?"

I didn't need to turn around to know that it was Lilah, half because it was such a Lilah thing to say, and half because I could see several purple strings flying around me in many directions. Obviously, I wasn't being quite as low-key about being caught in a mess of aura strings as I had hoped. Since no one else could see the strings, I must have looked pretty weird.

I hated my stupid Sight.

I opened my mouth to answer her hissed words of wisdom, but Lilah didn't want to hear it. "Do you want my help or don't you?"

This time, the "loser" part of her sentence went unstated.

"Lilah, I'm not sure what you're—"

"Listen, I don't have time for this. All I'm saying is that if you don't want to be Non-ed for life, then you better start acting like it, because there's only so much I can do. You want to hang out with the freaks? Fine, but if you're going to walk around here, hanging out with people like that and stumbling around with wide eyes like you're some kind of schizoid, don't come crying to me when you realize that you'll never be anyone at this school. If, on the other hand, you'd like to salvage what's left of your social life, let me know, and I'll see what I can do. Otherwise, you and your freakazoid friends can just stay out of my way."

With those words, she pushed by me in a huff, thoroughly pretending that she'd never seen me before in her life.

I stared straight ahead and walked into the building, ignoring the thousands of strings of light that I saw all around me. I was beginning to feel claustrophobic. Watching Lilah as she flounced down the hall and straight into Brock, I couldn't help but notice that they were connected, a dark blue rope of light running out from his aura to join with a purple light from hers. I squinted my eyes to look at the connection more closely, but I was too far away to see it very well.

Was that what I was seeing? I wondered. The connections between people? This was certainly an interesting development. With my eyes on the little strings of light, I tripped again, and flew straight into an encore performance of the Herald of Freakdom Incident.

Stupid Sight. Stupid connections. Stupid Lilah, just for good measure.

Sitting there on the hallway floor, I lifted my head just in time to see bottle-blond Tracy walk by. Snaking after her and whizzing straight by my face was a very thin string of noncolored light. Pinpricks spread across the back of my neck, and I swallowed hard.

Garn.

I squinted my eyes, forcing myself to look for its source, but in that instant, the stream of Garn recoiled, snapping like a rubber band back down the hallway and out of sight.

"What are you looking at, freak?" Tracy wasn't quite as subtle in her insults as Lilah was.

"Nothing," I said, standing up and looking down at my shoes. What had I seen? It wasn't a connection, not like the others. I seriously doubted Garn was capable of connecting with anything. Not even purple.

Grams had promised that I would see. Well, I was seeing now, and whether I liked it or not, I had a feeling that I was going to have to keep an eye on Tracy Hillard.

5

pearl

By the time I'd settled into my seat in history class, I was wondering if I'd really seen anything at all. Garn didn't just whiz down hallways. It was a little too evil for that. I was pretty sure that as a general rule, evil things didn't whiz. Then again, until today, auras hadn't tied themselves into neat little connections, and I hadn't been classified as a pathetic, desperate freak. Things changed.

People filed into the room, and I could see in their auras the exact moment they realized that there was a new kid. Their lights quivered or waved or stretched curiously in my direction. None of them said a word to me, so I sat there silently, trying to decode what their auras were telling me and trying not to think about the fact that the seats near me were staying obviously and horribly empty.

A few auras reached out toward me, spindles weaving their way cautiously through the air. Who was I? Did I bite? Three girls with glasses smiled tentatively in my direction and moved awkwardly around the desks toward the open seats next to me. Red, green, and blue spindles moved toward me a little hesitantly, and, like a person coaxing a scared puppy out from underneath a car, I smiled at them. One moment they were smiling warmly back at me, and the next, all their aura strings were quickly retracted back into their bodies, and without so much as another look in my direction, the girls turned on their heels and sat on the other side of the room. Their strings had moved so quickly that I couldn't help but think of someone touching a stove and pulling their hand immediately and frantically back.

Following the girls' nervous stares to the other side of the room, I swung my head slowly around and tried not to think about the fact that, though the rest of the room was filling up quickly, no one was sitting anywhere near me.

As I turned, I caught a glimpse of another aura string slithering my way, headed for my feet. I followed the trail of the string back to a girl with a mass of auburn hair. One look at her perfectly plucked eyebrows and the way her rose pink aura (which, by the way, clashed horribly with her hair) took up half the space in the room told me that she was a Golden, and when I caught the way she was raising her eyebrows at the girls who had almost sat next to me, I knew exactly what had happened.

She was giving me the social freeze. Probably on Tracy's orders, or Fuchsia's, or maybe just based on my own performance on the lawn. Right about now, Lilah's offer of social salvation, even on her terms, was starting to look pretty good.

Bad Lissy, my inner voice said. *Have you no pride?*

No one's sitting next to me, I replied silently. *No one. Nada. Zippo. The Big Oh . . .*

Calm down.

I met the redhead's eyes, and she smiled at me, sweetly. Warily, I watched pieces of her aura snake their way toward me. With my luck, they were probably going to tie me up or choke me to death or something, but instead, at the last instant, the pink cords changed directions. Without thinking, I swung my head around, following the movement.

There, standing in the doorway, were the first two familiar faces I'd seen since coming into this classroom. Two strong faces with well-sculpted chins. Two strong faces with well-sculpted chins that were headed in my direction. I noticed the blue lights before I saw the smirk on Brock's face, and as he slid into the chair behind me and to my left, Tate at his heels, I smiled at him. The connection between the two of them was thick and seamless, Brock's dark blue blending into Tate's golden. From the connection, I assumed that they were friends, and good friends at that.

Tate slid into the seat right behind me. Brock was conveniently positioned directly between me and the red-haired Golden.

Grateful, I turned to him. "Thanks," I said.

He stared at me as if trying to remember (a) if he knew me and (b) if I was worth talking to.

"I mean, hey, how's it going?" I was a brilliant conversationalist.

Brock just raised one eyebrow a bit, in a look that clearly expressed his bewilderment at why exactly I was looking at him in the first place.

"Hey," Tate replied, speaking for his friend, and that was all I got out of the two of them before they leaned back in their seats, their legs hanging into the aisles, clearly too cool for words.

I bit the inside of my lower lip and concentrated on not feeling so conspicuous. Half the seats next to me were still empty, the redhead was glaring at me for so much as having said a word to the boys, and if I had to see one more pink or purple aura circling around me like a hawk around its prey, I was going to puke.

One by one, I examined the colored streams of light in the room—anything to take my mind off the way the redhead and her friends (it figured that she had friends) were still giving the evil eye to anyone who tried to sit next to me.

Project Normal? I thought. Forget Project Normal. I wanted Project Find a Way to Make Someone Sit Next to Me. Taking a deep breath, I concentrated, really put everything out of my mind and concentrated on the spider's web of aura strings all around me.

A lot of the kids were connected to each other, which made sense, since they were probably friends. The cords of light were all different sizes, some as thin as floss and others as thick as a marker. Over in the corner, pink light melded seamlessly into green, and by the door, a girl and a boy were joined by what looked like a firmly tied knot.

Why a knot? I wondered. Why not the same seamless connection the others had? The girl slid her hand into the boy's, and in that moment, it clicked in my mind. They were dating, hence the knot. With the amount of time most high school relationships lasted, it made sense. A knot could be untied a lot more easily than the friendship cord could be broken.

But why a Garn stream of light in the hallway? Garn didn't have friends; Garn didn't have girlfriends. So why did it stream at all, and who did it belong to? I shook my head to clear it of unwanted thoughts. And why was it chasing Tracy? My inner voice insisted I consider the question, but since I had no answer and since Tracy had called me a freak, I valiantly ignored it and turned my attention back to the other students in the classroom.

Sneaking a peek at my own powder blue aura, I was disappointed to find that I wasn't connected to anyone in the class. Secretly, I'd been hoping for some sort of connection with Tate. After all, he'd hit me with a football, and he'd said hey, even when Brock had said nothing. That had to count for something, right?

Apparently not. I was the new girl, and it looked like

62

instant connections were hard to come by. I was really glad when the teacher started talking, because I'd had just about my fill of Golden guys who thought they were all that and couldn't be bothered with me other than to say "hey" now that they weren't pegging me in the head with footballs, and Nons who were too scared of pinky the redhead over there to sit anywhere near me.

Uggggg, I thought the second the word "Non" entered my mental vocabulary. I was becoming one of them.

"Hi, folks," the teacher boomed, his voice loud and clear. In the small classroom, it bounced off the walls and echoed slightly. It was like taking history in surround sound. "Today is our first day of a year together, a wonderful year during which we'll travel through time, from the colonial period up to now. We'll meet the likes of Paul Revere and Millard Fillmore, and . . ."

About that time, I stopped paying attention. I hated history more than any other subject. Everyone had to draw a line somewhere, and I drew the line at Millard Fillmore, whoever that was. As the teacher spoke, I watched his aura flow and his body language. He was gesturing madly, as if his hands couldn't stand still in the face of the excitement that was American history. His aura quivered with enthusiasm, and I wondered how anyone could get that excited over the Millard Fillmores of U.S. history.

". . . and then," he continued, "we'll move on to the Great Depression. Imagine, if you will, what it must have been like to live in those days." He paused for a moment, and I suddenly got a mental image of him jumping onto the table and tap-dancing at the thought of the Great Depression. That led me to thinking about dream Grams getting her groove on, which simultaneously disturbed me and made Grams' words from that morning hop into my head.

You'll see.

Furiously, I pushed the words out of my mind. She'd had to say them on my first day of school. Crazy old woman.

Smiling winningly, the teacher calmed down a bit and passed around a syllabus. Looking down, I discovered that his name was Mr. Wood, and I thought about how ill-suited he was to the name. He wasn't stern or unmoving like I pictured a Mr. Wood being. He was more like a Mr. Go-with-the-flow.

Beside me, Brock rolled his eyes a little, and I tried to catch his gaze and do the same. I managed it, and he didn't look at me oddly this time, but when I glanced down, I saw that there was still no connection between us whatsoever. Apparently, the little colored connector strings of light were based on more than just mutual feelings toward a history teacher.

"Now I know this may all seem a little over the top to you," Mr. Wood said, shrugging his shoulders in apology for his enthusiasm, "but I really do find it all absolutely fascinating." His aura had stopped quivering, but the green color was still moving at a fairly good pace, more smoothly than before.

Looking around the classroom, I realized that though Mr. Wood was completely over the top, at least half the class had been reluctantly caught up in his excitement, and tentative connections between students and teacher were already being formed.

Despite the fact that I kind of liked Mr. Wood, I hadn't formed a connection with him yet.

What was I? Connection deficient? So far, I'd only formed connections with Lilah and Audra. Granted, I was the new girl, but still. It seemed like I should have been getting at the very least a few exploring strings in my general direction. Then again, considering the fact that even sitting next to me was taboo, I wasn't terribly surprised.

"Let's just dive on into lecture," Mr. Wood said.

I took out a pen and paper, ready to take notes, even if it meant forcing myself to pay attention to his booming words instead of just watching his lights move as he talked.

I jumped in my chair when I felt a poke in my side.

"Can I borrow a pen?" Brock asked me. I dug through my bag and handed him a pen, wondering who came to school without any writing utensils.

"Thanks," he said, taking off the cap and lazily scrawling down a few notes. I forced myself not to glance down between us. Something told me that pen borrowing was not enough to forge a connection either, and when my entire visual field was almost overcome by an angry wave of pink and purple, I deduced that the Golden girls in the class considered pen loaning a grade-A felony and yet further confirmation that I was a pathetic, desperate freak.

Don't pay attention to them, my inner voice advised. *Listen to the teacher.*

For once, I gladly obeyed. Mr. Wood lectured question-and-answer-style, but he usually ended up being the person who asked *and* answered the question, half because no one in the class knew or felt compelled to volunteer the answer, and half because he couldn't slow down long enough to let someone else answer.

"And who was John Adams' cousin?" he asked, pacing the front of the room as he spoke.

I had no idea. My best guess was Abraham Lincoln.

"Sam Adams," Mr. Wood said, without stopping. "Sam Adams, one of the leaders of the rebellion. And what did Adams think of his cousin not only running with, but also leading, the rabble?"

The bell rang then, and Mr. Wood looked incredibly disappointed when everyone stood up to leave.

"I guess you all will just have to wait until tomorrow to find out," he said, as if the wait was going to be really, really hard.

As I gathered my books to leave, something flashed by the door.

Garn.

Holding back the tears that wanted to come to my

eyes just looking at that awful, awful aura stream, I pushed my way past the other students and hurried toward the hallway just in time to see a brassy blond head bob out of sight. I glanced up and down the hallway. No sign of anyone with a Garn-streaked aura.

I stared after Tracy for a moment. Even though she was gone, purple strings streamed around the corner, and one of them went right by my head. As Tate came out of the classroom, I looked at the bond between his yellow and her purple. The purple cord of light was wrapped around one of Tate's strings with a loose knot. A very loose knot.

Concentrate, my inner voice said. *Garn, remember? Forget about their love connection.*

Lack of love connection from the looks of it, I replied silently. *Besides, I'm not about to go looking for Garn. It's the worst thing ever, remember? Call me crazy, but I'd like my first day of school to involve as little of the worst thing ever as humanly possible.*

Determined not to lose another argument with my conscience and desperately clinging to Project Normal as much as I could with the lightcapades going on around me, I pulled out my schedule. As I did, I felt someone brush past me roughly. All I had to do was catch sight of three girls in miniskirts to deduce that I'd received my first physical snubbing. Today was turning out to be a really productive day in terms of social alienation. I mean, I seriously had to be setting records or something.

My teeth gritted, I made my way to my Spanish class, praying that someone, anyone, would sit next to me. Before I entered the room, I took one last look around the hallway to appease my conscience and, satisfied that there was no trace of the Garn stream, ducked into Spanish. From somewhere near the middle of the classroom, Audra waved to me.

Looking down at the thin connection between her peach aura and my currently baby blue one, I slid into the seat next to her with an audible sigh of relief.

"Hey," she said casually, giving me a small smile. "How goes it?"

"It?"

She nodded almost imperceptibly. "It."

"It goes badly," I said darkly. "History."

"History?" Audra asked, waiting for me to elaborate.

"U.S. history," I confirmed.

Audra wrinkled her forehead. "That's a junior class. Sophomores take European history."

"I took Euro last year at my old school," I explained. "And I haven't taken U.S. history yet, so they stuck me in with the juniors."

"And if it's a junior class . . ." Audra winced, her mind whirling. "Junior Goldens. Was Tracy there?"

I shook my head. "Nope."

"Did they keep everyone from sitting next to you anyway?"

"Yup."

She sounded so calm about it. Was this something that happened on a regular basis here? And how had I become a part of it so quickly? I was fly-under-the-radar, not-popular, not-unpopular girl. That was what I did. It was who I was.

"That's unfortunate," Audra said, "but at least you're in sophomore Spanish with yours truly. Hopefully that'll make things start going a little more smoothly."

In response to that comment, someone snorted. I turned my head toward the side and saw a guy who looked slightly familiar. I'd seen him in the yard earlier that day and noticed his firm friendship connection to Audra. He was on the thin side, and his hair desperately needed to be cut. Even as he spoke, he didn't look up at me.

"I'm Lissy," I said in my best friendly-but-not-flirty voice. I swore to myself that if he said hey and then ignored me, I would kill him. Slowly and painfully.

"I know," the boy replied, still not bothering to meet my eyes and sounding halfway between broody and bored. I looked to Audra for help, feeling a little irritated with this guy. It wasn't as if he was particularly good-looking, and he definitely wasn't a Golden, so why was he ignoring me almost completely? Had the Ignore Lissy memo really spread that quickly? Audra certainly wasn't the type to take that kind of thing seriously, and I had a hard time believing that her friend was, but still . . .

"This is Dylan," Audra said. "He's ugly and mean, but

he does a killer malnourished prairie dog impression, so we keep him around."

A smile played around the corner of his lips, and I had to disagree with Audra on one point. Dylan wasn't hideous-looking, if a person was into the broody, no-eye-contact kind of thing.

Remembering something, I leaned forward to ask Audra, in what I hoped was a casual voice, "Tracy and Tate—how long have they been going out?" Project Normal didn't extend quite so far that I was willing to forget about the little piece of aura gossip I'd picked up on that suggested that their time as a couple was limited. It was kind of ironic: I hadn't been at all interested in Tate to begin with, but ever since Tracy had flown into mondo-bitch mode the first time I'd talked to him, the idea of the two of them breaking up was growing on me.

"Too long," Audra replied under her breath. "It won't last another two months, though I pity the girl who gets him next." Beside me, Dylan snorted. "Tracy will make what they're doing to you look like spa day or something," Audra continued, ignoring him.

"And it starts again," Dylan said, lifting his head just slightly.

For a moment, I stared at him. I'd been so busy being irritated with him that I hadn't noticed that I couldn't tell what color his aura was. I could see the light shining off his skin, but it was pulled so closely to his body that I couldn't tell what color it was.

"What starts again?" I asked absentmindedly.

"*Español!*" the teacher enunciated, clapping her hands sharply in front of my face.

I stared at her. She clapped again.

"*Habla español,*" she said patiently.

"I don't speak—" I started to explain. She cut me off.

"*Español,*" she reminded me.

"*No español,*" I said, trying to explain to her that I didn't know how to say anything else and that I'd been signed up for Spanish class without my consent. She tilted her head to the side for a minute, looking at me, and then burst into happy laughter.

"*Que mono,*" she said, patting the top of my head.

"What's going on?" I whispered to Audra as soon as the crazy señora had turned her back.

"Don't ask me," Audra said. "I don't speak Spanish."

"*Español,*" the teacher reminded her firmly, skipping to the front of the classroom.

"Felicia," she said, looking straight at me. Fe-lee-see-ah. I went out on a limb and guessed that that was supposed to be my name.

I looked up at her. She chuckled.

"*Que mono,*" she said again. Then she continued to babble to me in Spanish.

I didn't even have to turn my head to know that Dylan was smirking beside me. I had a feeling that the smirk was his trademark expression.

Breaking into a grin, he looked toward me, and as he

spoke, I stared openmouthed at the lights surrounding his body.

"She either just said you're cute or that you look like a monkey," he offered. "I'm not really sure which." From the way he said the words, I was pretty sure that he was voting for the latter, but I was too busy trying to decide what was going on with his aura to pay much notice.

It shined out from his face as if coming out of his very pores, and it wasn't concentrated color or light like most auras were. Instead, it was almost a prism, sheer but full of many different colors. The light just shined softly from his face and faded as it traveled farther away.

Seeing soul light in its purest form made me feel like I was dreaming. *A silver shield.*

Struggling to see past the colors and the images in my mind, I stared at Dylan. The smirk had settled back over his mouth, and his eyes were set to brood mode. His colors didn't match his oh-so-charming personality at all.

By the end of the class period, I'd snuck several more looks at Dylan, who was connected to no one except for Audra, her peach melting into a pearly white strand that ran into his waist. I'd also listened attentively, or something like it, to the teacher, who didn't speak a word of English the entire class period and had yelled the word *"español"* gaily in my face 14.2 times.

As I walked out of the classroom, I heard a voice whisper in my ear. "Not too quick of a study, are you?"

I turned around to glare at Dylan. "What are you talking about?"

"*Español,*" he said seriously. Behind him, Audra started cracking up.

"You got *español*ed a lot more than the rest of us," she pointed out.

"Are all the teachers here this nuts?" I asked.

Dylan narrowed his eyes at me. "Sorry, Cali," he said, "but you're not in L.A. anymore." The way he said it made me feel like I was listening to fingernails on a chalkboard, and I couldn't seem to stop staring at his light-exuding face. I wanted, irrationally, to smack that cocky expression out of his eyes. Maybe it was because he was talking about California the same way Tracy had that morning. I couldn't help but think that every movie I'd ever seen had steered me totally and completely wrong. The new girl from California was supposed to be adored for her West Coast coolness, not mocked for it.

"What class do you guys have next?" Audra asked, breaking the silence that had fallen as Dylan and I stared at each other, each intensely annoyed.

I looked down at my schedule. "Wellness," I said. "What the heck is Wellness?"

Dylan shot me a mocking look when I said the word "heck," and I found myself mad that I'd said it in the first place. I was almost sixteen, not eight.

"Wellness is the school's attempt at making sure we all have our heads screwed on straight. It covers a little bit of biology, psychology, and plenty of touchy-feely role-playing games." Audra's voice turned singsongy.

I couldn't believe there was even such a class. What kind of school was this anyway?

"I have Wellness next too," Audra said. "All freshmen and sophomores take it."

"No juniors?" I asked.

"No juniors," Audra said.

Dylan stalked off without saying a word. Apparently a goodbye was more than Boy Wonder, the brooding-slash-smirking marvel, could manage. I stared after him as he left, not believing what I saw. Two pearl-colored streams of light trailed behind him, one connecting him firmly to Audra, and one connecting him to me.

He'd done nothing but grunt at me, and I knew for a fact that I didn't like him, and yet, we were connected. It was just my luck that the random connection fairy would have decided to screw me over with broody boy when Tate had been much nicer to me the day before, when he'd smacked me in the head with the football.

"So what about Tate?" I asked, my thoughts coming straight out of my mouth.

"What about him?" Audra asked, stopping at her locker. I noticed that it didn't have any locks on it, but then again, my parents hadn't even bothered locking our house this morning, and I couldn't really imagine anyone wanting to steal Audra's European history book.

"What do you think about him?" I asked, watching her carefully. My gut instinct and the way her aura stretched toward his whenever she looked at him told me that there was a distinct possibility that she liked him. The last thing I wanted was to crash my new friend's crush party. Then again, I felt halfway compelled to warn her that crushing on Tate could very well put her life in danger. Tracy didn't take competition well.

"I think that he'd look quite fetching in swim trunks, that he's reasonably nice for a Golden, and that he has the IQ of my pet goat's squeaky toy," she said, never pausing to take a breath and closing her locker door.

"You have a pet goat?" I asked, thinking that maybe my ideas about Oklahoma hadn't been completely misplaced.

She raised one eyebrow, and I felt like a complete idiot. "Of course not," she said, "but that's beside the point."

Together, the two of us walked into the Wellness classroom, and I was immediately overcome by a swarm of purple lights.

"I thought you said there weren't any juniors," I whispered.

Audra smiled with half her face as we slid into seats on the opposite side of the room. "There aren't," she whispered back, gesturing with her head toward the purple, pink, and teal girls sitting at the edge of the room, raising their eyebrows at me. The synchronized eyebrow raise: it was a new height in girl scare tactics. "Those are the sophomore Goldens."

It hadn't even occurred to me that some of the

Goldens were probably my age. I'd been having enough problems with the older ones. The idea of dealing with a mini-Lilah or a mini-Tracy was so not appealing.

"Who can define wellness?" an emotionless female voice asked. I looked toward the voice's source. At least this teacher appeared normal, or as normal as I could expect someone teaching Wellness to be.

Wellness, I said silently, *is being able to live your life without feeling like your head is going to explode and without wishing that it would. Wellness is not living in a place where you never know whether or not people are kidding about their pet goats. Wellness is not being only remotely connected to three people in your entire school, two of whom you don't like at all. Wellness is not getting* español*ed, or going into Paul withdrawal. Wellness is not being hated by half the high school and avoided by the other half.*

Wellness, my inner voice added, *isn't ignoring something that you know deep down is important. Ahem. Garn. Ahem, ahem.*

I looked at my watch. My conscience always got really cranky around lunchtime. Hopefully, if I ate something soon, it would shut up, and I could stop thinking about Tracy Hillard and her evil junior girl mafia and start thinking about something a little more appetizing.

6

brown

"Finally," I said when we broke for lunch. "Hallelujah." Audra grinned at me. The connection between us pulsed, my colors melting into hers and the connection growing thicker by the second.

"And on the third day," Audra quipped, "God said, 'Let there be food.'"

I cracked up, and even when one of the other girls sniffed at me, clearly too good for this kind of sarcastic banter, I ignored the way her aura lashed out at us. Watching the darting, constant movement of the Goldens' auras, I was quickly learning that nothing was ever quite as it appeared. A sniff was a dis, a smile was a warning, and touching a guy's hair was the Golden girl equivalent of a dog peeing on a tree to mark its territory.

As we walked out of the classroom, my stomach rumbled. Loudly.

"Hungry much?" Audra asked, her peach lights wiggling in tune with her teasing voice. I nodded, and this time, I didn't even have to look at the purple auras pulling away from me to know what the sophomore Goldens thought of my too-loud stomach.

"Starved," I said, looking down at the connection between Audra and me. "Lead the way." Obligingly, Audra turned a corner and walked at a good pace to the cafeteria. I followed her, and without meaning to, I glanced around the cafeteria. Colored strings of light pulsed and pulled and twisted. For a split second after I walked into the room, all the movement stopped as everyone in the entire room turned to look at me at once. There were pointed stares and curious stares and a few I-can't-believe-she's-wearing-those-shoes-with-that-shirt stares, but they were all looking at me, and the blood rushed to my face.

Careful. They can smell fear, my inner voice warned.

A split second later, when the auras started to move again, I wondered if I had imagined it. Audra's words convinced me that I hadn't.

"New girl factor," she explained. "Most people here have gone to school together their whole lives. You would have gotten the new girl stare even if Tracy hadn't sent out the persona non grata memo."

I didn't know the exact meaning of the phrase, but I got the drift. "They have memos?" I asked weakly, only half joking. At a school where people had to match their shoe choice to their level of coolness to avoid ridicule, I wasn't completely sure that there weren't memos.

"Evil memos," Audra confirmed with a straight face. I grinned. Somehow, hanging out with Audra made wading through a mess of royally bold aura colors almost bearable. As I walked up to the serving line, I couldn't help but glance over my shoulder. Bubblegum pink, purple, tennis ball yellow, red, green . . . The room was crowded with auras, but there was no Garn in sight. Turning my mind back to the lunch-picking task at hand, I tried to inconspicuously examine the hot food.

I wrinkled my nose, and inconspicuousness flew out the window.

"Trust me, you don't want to eat that," Audra said. "Unless you're in favor of cannibalism?"

I shook my head, even though I knew she was joking.

"Grab a sandwich, some chips, and a milkshake," she told me.

Milkshake? I smiled. I was a big fan of all things ice cream–related. Picking up a chocolate shake and a sandwich that looked only mildly sketchy, I maneuvered my way to the cashier, digging some money out of my pocket as I walked.

Paying for my meal, I caught sight of Brock and Lilah coming through the line. Lilah's head was tilted slightly to the side, and every once in a while, her lips parted to reveal pearly white teeth in a flirty smile. Her fingertips played with the ends of her dark hair, and every time

Brock tried to look away from her, I swear she hiked her already short skirt up another inch. Pretty soon, she was going to be mooning the guy serving the sloppy joes.

Trying to think of something other than this less-than-pretty scenario, I noticed that Lilah had nothing on her tray except for two milkshakes, and that Brock had enough food to feed a small army on his. Trying not to stare, I examined what I could see of the connection between them, thoroughly ignoring it when she pulled on the edge of her top, exposing more of her chest than her V-neck shirt already had. She had Brock's full attention now.

Their connection tightened as he took a step toward her. It was about as thick around as a pencil, and when he moved closer to her (or, more accurately, when he moved closer to her breasts), the excess light disappeared into her aura.

The purple string extending from her lights was tightly knotted to his Paul-colored string. Maybe it was wishful thinking, but I thought it looked like the knot was her string tied around his. I figured that connections were open to interpretation, and my interpretation was that the Lilah-heavy knot meant that Lilah was more into Brock than Brock was into her.

Stop thinking like that, my inner voice scolded me.

I ignored the voice and managed to tear my eyes away from the two of them.

"Come on," Audra said, pulling my elbow toward an

empty table. I followed her, my inner voice keeping up a mantra discouraging me from dropping my tray.

Don't drop your tray. Don't drop your tray.

Successfully sitting down at the lunch table without dropping my tray, I leaned back in my chair a little and looked around. The lunchroom was absolutely brimming with people, their auras competing for space in my mind.

"Is this everyone?" I asked. I glanced from table to table. Why was I not surprised that there was a clear physical separation between the Goldens on one side of the cafeteria and the Nons on the other? It was like a scene out of *West Side Story* or something. I half expected the two groups to get up and start dancing/fighting with catchy choreography and lyrics about who was hot (or hotter or hottest) and who was not.

Tearing my mind away from that little mental image, I continued scanning the cafeteria. No Garn. This couldn't be everyone, not if I couldn't find the Garn person. Why was I so obsessed with finding the owner of that Garn stream anyway? Seeing an aura with even the tiniest streak of Garn always hit me like a punch in the stomach. What was I, some kind of masochist?

Stupid conscience.

"Well, now everyone's here," Audra said, looking just over my shoulder.

Silently and without so much as sparing me a glance, Dylan sat down. Taking a drink of my milkshake, I ignored the pearly white string that extended from his body toward me. I was in connection denial, and as far as I was concerned, broody boy and I were just acquaintances.

"Hey," he said in a low voice, immediately starting to eat.

I rolled my eyes, not sure what it was about him that rubbed me the wrong way. The three of us ate in silence for a while, and I took the opportunity to check out the rest of the kids sitting with Lilah. I recognized the redhead from U.S. history talking to Fuchsia. After a moment, Fuchsia cut the girl off and flounced over to sit next to Lilah. I couldn't help but take pleasure in the fact that the girl who had kept everyone from sitting next to me in history class obviously wasn't on Fuchsia's hottest list. Served her right.

The spastic and jerky movement of her bright purple aura drew my attention to Tracy, who was frowning fiercely in the general direction of her boyfriend. Apparently, there was trouble in Tracy-Tate land. Even from this distance, I could see the knot that connected them slowly untying. I turned my attention back to my food. In my opinion, a relationship between a purple and a golden yellow was never meant to last. The colors didn't blend well, their personalities didn't complement each other well, and honestly, purple was the color of a she-devil.

Telling myself that I was just watching out in case there was a break in the Garn stream case, I stared at the connection between the two Goldens, and I felt myself being drawn in. Suddenly, the connection appeared closer than before, and I could see the knot in great detail. Tracy's string was taut with her body, Tate's loose, and as he moved around the table to say something to Brock and Lilah, his side of the connection became even more lax.

Completely entranced, I left logic far behind and lifted my hand to touch the knot, wondering what it would feel like, even though I knew quite well that I wouldn't be able to touch it. I was too far away, and auras weren't tangible in the first place.

I blinked as I saw the outline of a hand reach slowly toward the string. If I hadn't known better, I would have thought it was a ghost's hand, because I could see straight through it, and the sight sent a shiver up my spine. I looked down at my own hand and discovered that it hadn't moved at all. That was odd. I could have sworn that I'd been moving my hand.

I tried to move it again, and the ghost hand moved in front of my eyes. Blinking again, I saw the hand connected to the outline of a body. My body. There, on the other side of the cafeteria, my ghost self stood, mere inches away from the connection between Tracy and Tate.

My real eyes widened, but without stopping to think, because I wasn't exactly a think-y kind of girl, I reached out with my ghost hand to touch the knot between Tracy and Tate. The connection was pleasantly cool to the touch, a string-sized ice cube on a hot summer day. Under my touch, the connection trembled, and I felt the knot slip just a little bit more.

In the corner of my eye, I saw the smallest flash of horrible light, devoid of all color, and it snapped me back into my body. Garn. Immediately, I scanned the lunchroom, trying not to feel ridiculous for playing hide-and-seek with an aura.

"Tate!" Tracy's high-pitched voice cut across the cafeteria.

"Trouble in paradise," Audra commented, nodding her head toward Lilah's table, where Tracy and Tate were entering into some kind of argument.

If I could just find the string, I could follow it to its owner. Maybe it was just my conscience, maybe it was my intuition, but I couldn't shake the horrible need to know where the Garn was coming from.

"Darn my mortal ears," Audra said, breaking my concentration. "I can't tell what they're saying."

"The fact that you care . . . ," Dylan said, shaking his head and cutting off his words with a shrug.

Audra responded with a shrug of her own. "I don't think they're good together," she admitted freely.

Dylan arched an eyebrow and looked at her from underneath his too-long hair. "And he'd be better with you?" he asked.

"No," Audra said vehemently, but I noticed her aura

moving in tune with her heartbeat, a sure sign of crushage.

I squinted and looked out each of the windows in turn. Not knowing where the Garn was coming from or when it was going to show up again was like walking around knowing that any second, some guy with a knife was going to jump out and scare the Aura Vision right out of me.

I looked back at Tracy, wondering if the Garn stream would show again. The moment my eyes settled on their table, Tate turned an annoyed look on Tracy.

In my mind, I saw the way my ghost hand had nudged the knot on its slipping path. My real hands shook a little as I realized the implications. Tate and Tracy were well on their way to breaking up, quicker even than Audra thought, and it was due, in some part, to me.

On one level, this just didn't feel right. On another entirely separate level, it felt really, really, extremely cool, and hey, if you really thought about it, I was doing the world a social service. Every once in a while, girls like Tracy needed to lose. On a third and completely unre-lated level, it felt like something horrible was about to happen, and I didn't know why. If only I could find the stream, I could force myself to face down the nausea that a little bit of Garn would cause and get on with my life and the matchmaking possibilities in my future. If I could untie a connection, surely I could tie one as well.

The thought didn't cheer me up as much as it should have.

"What's with you?" Dylan asked. Instead of dishing out a sarcastic reply, I found myself staring at the light coming out of the front of his face. He had such an unusual aura that I couldn't help but look at it closely, and from the moment my eyes locked onto the light, I felt completely at ease for the first time since I'd seen the Garn stream that morning.

"Malnourished prairie dog . . . ," I said, snapping myself out of it and remembering the phrase Audra had coined in respect to Dylan's look. The moment I tore myself away from his pearl white aura, my eyes swept first back to Tracy and then to the window. No Garn.

"You are one strange girl," Dylan told me softly, not bothering to turn to look at me.

I looked at him, and for a moment, the anxiety subsided. "What do you mean?" I asked.

"You've barely eaten a thing," Audra said, explaining for her more silent counterpart, "you just spent a great deal of time staring out the window and then across at your cousin . . ."

"She's not my cousin," I said. *And I was staring at Tracy, not Lilah,* I added silently.

". . . and you completely left off in the middle of a sentence in which you were insulting Dylan," Audra finished.

I looked down at my hands, and the moment I looked

away from Dylan's aura, my heartbeat sped up. I tried to shake the feeling. It wasn't logical that I felt so on edge. I'd seen Garn before, but no matter how many times I told myself to calm down, all I could hear in my mind was my grandmother's voice playing over and over again.

You'll see.

"You just did it again," Audra said dryly.

"Did what?" I asked.

Audra sighed. "What's your last hour?" she asked, giving up on me finishing my Dylan insult.

I paused for a moment, trying to gather my thoughts. Project Normal was failing magnificently, and if I wasn't careful, this whole Garn stream thing was going to make the only person at school who was even remotely my friend think I was a total freak. "Precalculus," I said, answering her question.

Audra nodded her head toward Dylan. "Dyl's in that class," she said. "It's a junior class."

Oh goody.

Note to self, half of me thought, *stop taking advanced classes and you won't have to deal with the junior Goldens.* The other half of me was staring at Dylan's aura, trying to keep from going crazy and trying to keep Grams' words out of my head.

You'll see.

"Do you have Kissler for PC?" Audra asked. It took me a minute to catch on to the fact that by "PC" she meant precalc, and another minute to respond coherently.

"I don't know," I said, pulling my schedule out of my pocket and triumphantly ignoring the impulse to check the window for Garn again. "Let me see." After glaring at the part of my schedule that informed me that chorus was my next class, and checking my window impulse again, I nodded in response to Audra's question. I wasn't ready to give up on this "normal" thing yet.

"Do you think they'll break up today?" Audra asked again, glancing over at Tracy's table, unable to help herself. I took a deep breath and looked over there. No Garn.

"You're both hopeless," Dylan said, scarfing down the last bit of his third sandwich and wiping his hands off with a napkin.

Audra and I turned to look at him, identical expressions on our faces, only mine softened the moment the pearl white came into view.

"And the MPD has spoken," Audra pronounced majestically.

"MPD?" I asked, before realizing I knew just what it stood for: malnourished prairie dog.

I laughed and took another sip of my chocolate shake, only to find that I was already scraping the bottom of the glass. Discarding my sandwich as something that fit into the category of not-chocolate, I played with the idea of purchasing another shake. It seemed like a better use of my time than staring at Tracy and waiting for the Garn stream to show itself again, which I couldn't seem to help but do.

"You don't want any more ice cream," Audra advised

me. "Trust me, those shakes are really rich, and I don't know anyone who can drink two without getting completely nauseous."

"That sounds like a challenge," I said, and, desperate to move, to do something, I stood up and went to get another milkshake. Lilah had had two on her tray; therefore, I couldn't think of a single reason that I wouldn't be able to drink two of them. Besides, the sandwich really was pretty nasty.

After paying for my second chocolate shake, I grabbed some napkins from the dispenser, turned around, and ran straight into Tracy Hillard. I narrowly missed spilling chocolate all over her, and even though I would have paid big money to see her nice and chocolate-covered, I definitely didn't want to be the one to do the covering.

Immediately and without meaning to, I glanced quickly around in a Garn check. No Garn.

"Watch where you're going," she said coolly. "Some of us are trying to walk here."

Apparently, she was using the royal we.

"O-o-okay," I stammered, cursing myself for stammering. What reason did I possibly have to be afraid of her? She was just a normal girl, and not as powerful or as smart as Lilah was, so why did looking at her make me feel like crawling under a table? She was the one being chased by a Garn stream, and she was the one who'd nearly broken up with her boyfriend because of my knot-untying skills (and possibly because of the fact that he'd said hey to me during history class). I was the one who held her fate in my hands, not the other way around.

"Just stay out of my way," Tracy said dangerously. Then she laughed slightly and delicately arched one overplucked eyebrow as she looked at my hair. I could practically feel it frizzing as her eyes gave it a once-over.

Don't let her push you around, my inner voice said.

So now you're on my side, I thought. *What about earlier when you were all "no, don't do that to poor Tracy; it's wrong" and "ahem, Garn, ahem," huh?*

The voice said nothing, most likely because I couldn't think of anything for it to say.

"Do you mind?" Tracy asked, absolutely sneering at me.

Mind what? I wondered.

"What's your problem, Tracy?" a male voice asked from beside me. Looking over, I noticed that Tate had approached the two of us. His golden brown aura was gathered tightly to his body and loose around his head.

The entire area was still Garn-free.

I turned my attention to the connection between them. Tate's end of the string was slipping out of the knot and retracting back into his golden base aura. This was the beginning of the end for Tracy and Tate. His aura moved erratically, bouncing away from his body at odd times and then pulling back in tightly. He looked nervous.

Watching their auras, I wondered if this wasn't the main attraction, the event that was pulling me to watch Tracy over and over. Maybe it had nothing to do with that stupid little stream at all. Tate was being incredibly nice to stand up for me, even if he was just doing it to pick a fight with her, which I was pretty sure he was. He wanted to sever the knot, but he didn't want to be the bad guy. He was such a typical male.

Tracy glared at me and then turned sweetly to Tate. "We were just having some navigational problems," she said, a fake and musical laugh entering her singsongy voice. I figured that "navigational" was probably a pretty big word for her. The syrupy sweet tone in her voice made me lose all appetite for chocolate milkshakes and other edibles.

I looked back at Tate, knowing that he wouldn't be buying any of this, only to see that his aura had stopped moving and that the weak knot was again in place.

I looked over at Tracy. She was about to bust out of her tight shirt. Tate smiled a loopy grin at her. Guys were such complete and total idiots.

Tracy just looked at me, and as her aura hissed, I got the message loud and clear that I wasn't wanted.

Taking my milkshake back to the table, I sat down and firmly decided that I didn't care about the mystery Garn person. The owner of the Garn stream could eat Tracy, or any other Golden at this twisted school, for all I cared. Besides, it was completely possible that the Garn stream had nothing to do with Tracy, and that the fact that I'd seen it in her presence a couple of times was just a giant coincidence. I mean, maybe the streams followed their owner around, or maybe they just flew around randomly.

Or maybe, the stream was just a little piece of hatefulness waiting for the right time to embed itself in Tracy's aura.

"How does she do that?" Audra asked as I sat down. "All of a sudden, he's all over her again."

Dylan buried his head in his hands, the most expressive gesture I'd seen him make. I took that to mean he was sick and tired of Tate-centric conversations.

"It's a mystery," I said, taking a nice long drink of my milkshake and relishing that I didn't care anymore. "Girls like that are always a mystery."

Dylan gave us a wry look. "Breasts," he said flatly. "Status. Hookup." Audra and I looked at each other and shrugged. Apparently, to the male mind, it was a fairly simple equation.

"Eh," Audra said, and I got the feeling that she desperately wanted to change the subject. I didn't blame her. The Golden relationships weren't exactly appetizing fodder. She stood up. Following her lead, I went to throw my trash away just as I'd finished my second milkshake.

"Told you I could do it," I teased her triumphantly. I wasn't feeling any worse for the wear, and for the first time all day, the streams of Garn were the last thing on my mind.

Audra grinned, and just as I set my tray down, she pointed over my shoulder. "There's Mr. Kissler," she said. "Besides Tate and Brock, he's the best-looking guy in the school." She said it matter-of-factly, as if his being a teacher meant nothing on the cute-guy scale.

I turned to look, and what I saw took my breath away. Streams of Garn soared through the cafeteria, caressing the other auras, and all the lights shuddered under the touch of the hideous Garn aura tentacles.

"Isn't he gorgeous?" Audra asked. Behind her, Dylan groaned audibly.

I didn't say anything. My eyes locked on Mr. Kissler, and my legs froze to the ground, as heavy as lead. The feeling of horrible numbness spread up my body as I stared at him, unable to tear my eyes away.

His aura was broad, the spindles streaming off it almost all-encompassing. His entire aura was completely devoid of color, worse than colorless. It looked dead, as if it had never really been composed of light at all. It wasn't just a streak or two or three.

Mr. Kissler was entirely Garn.

Looking at that awful noncolor, I could feel the nausea rising in the back of my throat, and tears came to my eyes. My ears roared, and I couldn't breathe. Everything blurred, and the last thing I was aware of before I plunged into complete darkness was the fact that I'd just thrown up two chocolate milkshakes all over the floor.

7

garn

I was surrounded by darkness. Looking around, I could see nothing, but I could feel the wrongness of it all in the air. Why couldn't I see? I was blind and terrified, and the earth was shaking beneath me.

Then an unearthly light filled the space, and I saw a figure walking toward me, surrounded by a pale light of changing colors. I knew instinctively that the figure was a she, even though I could see no defining features. As she walked closer, the light became too bright for my eyes, accustomed to darkness, and I closed them, allowing her presence to push back the darkness.

With cool hands she touched my eyelids, and then I opened my eyes, the coolness still on my face. She was gone. Now I could see, but I wished that I couldn't. I was surrounded on all sides by walls the color of screams, frozen in a victim's throat.

"Aaaaaaagckkkkkkkkkkk!" I yelled, coughing and

sputtering as the nonsense word ripped cruelly through my raw throat. I opened my eyes and bolted up in bed.

Wait a second. Why was I in bed?

I blinked and looked around the room. The last thing I remembered, I had been at school, and now I had no idea where I was. I certainly wasn't home, in my bed facing the oceanside window.

"Lissy," a familiar voice said. I blinked again, and things finally came into complete focus. I was staring directly at my grandmother.

"Where am I?" I asked, my voice rough.

"Room," my grandmother replied in characteristic style, and I knew she meant that we were in my new bedroom, even though she didn't actually say it. I hadn't recognized the attic room. I still didn't even think of it as my room, really. My real room was back in California, at home.

"What happened?" I asked, trying desperately to figure out what was going on and why exactly I felt like I'd been hit by a train carrying Ebola.

Grams stared at me, touching the back of her hand to my forehead and making a *tsk*ing sound as she shook her head. The hand felt cool on my forehead, like I remembered the Tracy/Tate knot feeling to my hand.

"You need to tell me what happened, Lissy, my star," Grams said softly. I tried to remember.

"I was in a room," I told her, "and it was dark. Then there was light, a woman I think, and then it was awful."

Grams stared at me. "Not your dream, child," she said. "At school. What happened at school?"

I looked at her cluelessly. "What do you mean?"

"You fainted," she said, "and threw up. They called the house and your mother and father were out. I came to get you, and you came to for a moment, muttering some nonsense. Not a second after I got you into bed, you passed out again, convulsing and gagging."

That was a cheerful image.

"How did you get me up three flights of stairs?" I asked.

"I had help," Grams replied shortly, and I had a feeling I didn't want to know who the help was. It would have been just like her to order some passerby to carry me. How humiliating. Though not as humiliating as the fact that I'd apparently thrown up in the middle of the cafeteria.

"Concentrate, my light," Grams instructed, pulling another senseless nickname out of nowhere. "What made you so sick?"

I tried to remember, and it came to me in pieces. The connections I'd seen, the way I'd left my body to play with them, the fight Tate and Tracy had been having. Had there been something else about Tracy? I wasn't sure.

Just then, the door to my room flew open and my mom ran in, my dad following close behind. "Are you all right?" my mom asked, out of breath. My dad hung back

96

for a moment, standing in the doorway, his mouth tensed slightly, his aura wrinkling as it pulled to his face in unspoken worry.

I realized my mom was still waiting frantically for a reply, so I nodded.

She shuddered. "I saw you," she said, her voice almost broken. "Little and shaking."

As she spoke, the golden brown lights surrounding my dad's body stretched out toward hers. The connection between the two of them was as thick as my fist, and as his aura waved toward her in an effort to comfort, the connection grew, until golden brown met green in a wall of color that, for a moment, flashed pearly white.

My mom took a deep, soothing breath, and I wondered what other images she was banishing from her mind.

"Hush, Katie," Grams said gently, even though my mom wasn't saying anything anymore. "Tell us, Lissy. What happened?"

I thought hard. Audra and I had gone to put our trays away, and she'd turned to point someone out to me, the math teacher. The memory of his aura hit me like a cement truck, and I gagged in reflex.

"Tell!" Grams ordered. "What did you see?"

My dad slipped out of the room as soon as Grams brought up the Sight, but not before his aura moved gently toward me in a single, soothing motion.

"What?" Grams was back to one-word questions.

"Garn," I whispered, shivering.

Grams looked at me like I had three heads, but my mom understood me. "The color of nothingness," she told Grams. "It's something Lissy made up when she was little." She made it sound like Garn was the boogeyman or something.

"It's not something I made up," I said testily. "It's something I see."

Grams and Mom looked at each other. "You haven't seen Garn in years," my mother said gently. "Not since you stopped running into our room at night with nightmares and sleeping with a night-light on." The tone of her voice made it clear that she thought Garn had been banished with all my other childhood fears.

"I've always seen it," I said defensively. "Just not very often, and I don't like to talk about it, so I just never say anything, but I saw it today." My voice dropped down to almost a whisper. "Not a spot or a streak. A little Garn is bad enough, but . . ." I trailed off for a moment and then finished, "His aura was entirely Garn." I swallowed my desire to gag at the thought and forced the roaring sound out of my ears.

For people who put a lot of stock in the Sight, my mother and Grams were both acting like I was crazy for even mentioning Garn. Maybe if I'd named it something that sounded less silly, I would have had more luck with them, but the first time I'd seen Garn, I'd only been three, and the tiny sliver had forced me sobbing into my mother's arms. I hadn't given a lot of thought to naming it properly.

Just then, my uncle came into the room, walking briskly. He looked at my grandmother, annoyed. "You should have called me," he told her sternly, sounding as if he was the parent and she was the child instead of the other way around. "The school nurse called to let me know that you'd be bringing Lissy in soon, but you never came. My own niece comes down with some horrible mystery flu, and I'm the last to know."

He wasn't ranting. Uncle Corey didn't rant, but I could see the worry in the way his aura moved curtly around his body, the motion severely limited. He sat down beside my bed and put a hand on my forehead.

"Just a slight fever," he murmured, pulling a thermometer out of nowhere and sticking it into my mouth. I wondered why he didn't have one of those handy ear thermometers, but then I remembered that we were in Oklahoma.

"Don't go getting any ideas, girl," Grams said, chuckling. "That thermometer is just more portable." Apparently, ear thermometer technology *had* reached Oklahoma, and Grams could read my mind like a book. Oklahoma on the whole wasn't shaping up to be at all what I had imagined.

I tried to say something, but Uncle Corey silenced me with his stern doctor's look as he took a stethoscope out of a bag and carefully placed it against my chest.

"Your heart is racing," he told me. "Your breathing is constricted."

That was probably why I felt like I was about to implode any minute. (Exploding was so overrated. If I was going to be doing any ploding at all, it was going to be *im*ploding.)

"Are you sure about what you saw?" Grams asked, wrinkling her forehead a bit. I nodded, and Uncle Corey glared at us both.

"There's more," I told Grams. "Not about the Garn, but about my Sight. It's . . ." I searched for the right word. "Growing."

"Not you too," Uncle Corey said, looking down at me and shaking his head. "I swear that insanity runs in this family." He quickly corrected himself. "In the females of this family."

"I can see these strings connecting people," I said, feeling dumb at how absurd it sounded when spoken out loud.

Grams nodded, a thoughtful look crossing her face. She didn't seem terribly surprised, and it occurred to me for the second time that somehow, all this was probably Grams' fault.

Seeing connections, Grams' fault.

Weird dreams, Grams' fault.

Puking all over my shoes somehow had to be Grams' fault.

My little voice said nothing, and I assumed that meant my assumptions about blaming Grams were entirely accurate. Thinking about that made me dwell on the fact that I had thrown up in front of the entire school. How very promising for my social standing.

"I can never go to school again," I moaned.

Uncle Corey, well into his doctor role, stood up. "I think you'll be fine," he said. "You should be able to go back to school tomorrow, or possibly Wednesday at the latest."

I rolled my eyes and sank farther down into my bed. "You don't understand," I muttered. "I *can't* go back."

"Don't be ridiculous," Uncle Corey said. "I'm sure no one will hold you accountable for being ill. I know Lilah will be in your corner." He spoke about Lilah as if she was the absolute model of decorum and civility.

Yeah, right, I thought. With my luck, by Wednesday, Lilah, Tracy, and Fuchsia would probably have managed to somehow immortalize the moment my semblance of a life had dive-bombed. I could just see her passing out flyers or staging a reenactment.

Another thought occurred to me, a more obvious and pressing problem than the fact that I was now officially a certifiable freak. The Garn man (I couldn't call him anything else in my thoughts) was supposed to be my math teacher. I could hardly think about him without feeling like I was going to vomit. How in the world was I going to sit through his class?

To have an aura that stripped of color, he had to have done something horrible. More than that, he had to *be* someone horrible. Without any color at all in his aura, I didn't see how there could even be a trace of humanity in him. It was entirely possible he'd killed someone, or worse. To top it all off, I couldn't shake the feeling that I wasn't even seeing the whole, horrible picture, the feeling that I was missing something.

"I can't go back," I said again. I looked at my mom and Grams. "He's there." They looked at me blankly, and their auras darkened as if they'd stepped into the shade. "The Garn man," I said, feeling ridiculous. "He's my math teacher. I know you don't believe me, but I know my gift, and he's done something horrible." My voice cracked and I sat forward, feeling my heartbeat in my pounding headache.

"You're overexerting yourself," my uncle said, pushing me firmly back against the pillow and dismissing everything I said as crazy sight-talk.

"Your math teacher. Jonah Kissler?" Grams asked. Then she clucked her tongue. "He's a wonderful man, Lissy."

I stared at her, unbelieving. She was the one who had wanted me to embrace my gift. Well, about now, she could pretty much consider it embraced, because this time I was definitely listening to what my Sight was telling me.

"I know what I saw," I said. Why wouldn't they believe me? Grams and Mom especially should have known that I wouldn't lie about things like this, and that I'd been seeing auras long enough to know what it was that I was seeing.

102

"You know what you *think* you saw," Grams said in a kind, soft voice, her shadowy silver aura waving softly in rhythm with her words. "Your gift is still untrained, Lissy. You don't know how to interpret these things yet, and you can't separate your emotions fully from what you see."

I figured that was Grams' convoluted way of telling me that I was an ignorant child who didn't know what she was talking about.

"There is something wrong with that man," I said firmly, crossing my elbows over my chest, my heart finally slowing down. Being stubborn distracted me from the thought that I knew I'd never be able to look into a pure Garn aura and feel anything but a horrid and all-consuming emptiness.

"Jonah is a good man," my uncle said sternly. "I can't tell you how often he has volunteered his time at the hospital, and all the kids say he's a wonderful teacher. Emily is so upset that Lilah isn't taking one of his classes."

So we were back to Emily and Lilah. Next to Mr. Kissler, they were, of course, my favorite topic of conversation. I grunted in frustration, not caring if I sounded weird. With the shape his aura was in, there was a good chance that my math teacher hadn't just done something horrible. My every instinct told me that he was *doing* something horrible, something I'd have to look at every time I saw him. How was I supposed to concentrate on precalculus and variables when I knew he was going to make me physically ill just by being in the room?

"I can't take that class," I said firmly. "I'll throw up every time I see him. I'll shake, pass out, the works."

"Don't build yourself that kind of psychosis," my uncle said, his golden aura in what I liked to call its doctor position: moving gently, but in a restricted area. Strings thicker than any I'd seen so far connected my uncle to Grams and to my mom, and the two of them were connected as well. All three of them were connected to me. At least I wasn't completely connection-deficient. Then again, a connection drought was the least of my current problems.

"Your Sight doesn't control you," Grams said firmly, making Uncle Corey let out a frustrated grunt. "You control it."

I almost snorted. I had never controlled my Sight. "I won't take that class," I said flatly.

My mom gave me a look. "We'll talk when you feel better," she said, and I knew that was her way of saying that when I felt better, she'd tell me I had to take the class anyway. They were being ridiculous. Why didn't anyone believe me when I said there was something wrong with my math teacher?

As I sat there, feeling irritated with them, the connections between us tightened on my half, putting tension into the strings. From the way my mom's half was tightening as well, I inferred that she was probably getting just as annoyed with me. My "I'm Sick, Get Out of Jail Free" card had had a surprisingly short life span.

"I hear you threw up in school," Lexie said sympathetically as she came into the room.

"How did you hear that?" I asked. "You don't even go to the same school."

"Small town," my uncle said, repressing a smile. "Word travels fast." I glared at him. There was no world in which this was funny.

As Lexie pulled a still-full moving box over next to my bed and sat down on it, the adults started to leave the room. It was about time. If I had to listen to one more person telling me that there was nothing wrong with my math teacher, I was going to scream. Just thinking about his aura made the bile rise in the back of my throat.

"Don't think about it," Grams said as she left. "Sleep."

Argh, I thought.

"Argh," I said out loud.

"Think about what?" Lexie asked. I looked at her for a moment.

"Garn," I said finally, not really wanting to go through the whole explanation again.

Lexie nodded solemnly, even though she had no idea what I was talking about. Then she stared at me patiently, waiting for me to continue.

The whole story slipped out, at something close to terminal velocity. "My math teacher is evil, or something like it. His aura is devoid of color—worse than that, it's the very worst color. I've never seen so much of it, and every time I see it, I know that the person has done something horrible. It makes me sick just looking at it, and Lex, he's completely covered."

Lexie said nothing. She just listened.

"Compound that with the fact that my Sight has picked this opportunity to suddenly morph into letting me see the connections between people and the part where aforementioned awful aura made me puke in front of the entire school, and you've got my day in a nutshell."

"Your power is expanding?" Lexie asked, her voice half-curious and half-jealous. It figured that out of everything I'd said, that was what had drawn her attention the most.

"Focus, Lexie," I said.

She shrugged and offered me a small smile. "I believe you about the other part," she said. "Your teacher. There is something wrong with him. That's true." She said it so simply that, coming from her lips, it didn't sound nearly so crazy.

"Thanks, Lex," I said.

"What are you going to do?" she asked me, not pausing for a moment. Lexie always moved at warp speed.

"Do?" I asked. "I'm going to try to find a way out of that math class, or better yet, I'm going to find a way out of this town and back to Cali where I belong." That sounded like a good plan.

"But if he's doing something horrible," Lexie said

logically, "how can you just leave? You wouldn't be seeing it if you weren't supposed to do something."

Lexie didn't understand that my Sight wasn't like some kind of television superpower on the teen soap network. I couldn't do anything with it. I just watched on the sidelines.

I told her so.

"That's not true," she said.

"How would you know?" I asked her. She just stared at me with round, hurt eyes, and I felt awful. If there was one thing Lexie was sensitive about, it was not having the Sight, and I'd just thrown it in her face.

"I did do something today," I told her, offering her a peace branch. Glancing at the door to make sure my mother and grandmother weren't anywhere close by, I explained the way Tate and Tracy had been connected, the way I'd left my body, and the way my ghost hand had helped the knot on its way to becoming untied.

She stared at me, and I knew I was forgiven. "Wow," she said, "just wow." She paused for a moment and then sighed. "It's really not fair, you know," she told me amiably. "Now, all of a sudden, you can see auras, you can see connections, *and* you can leave your body and play with the connections. Is it just me, or did you get my share of Sight in addition to yours?"

I didn't know quite what to say to that. I opened my mouth to tell her that I would have gladly traded places with her, given that she hadn't had to sit by herself in history, and that she hadn't just thrown up all over her shoes in front of the entire student body on the first day of school, but as soon as I opened my mouth to speak, another figure entered the room.

At first, I couldn't tell who it was because of the way the light from the hallway blurred her image in my eyes, and an image of the woman in my dream jumped into my head.

"Hi," a not-so-thrilled voice said.

"Hey, Lilah," Lexie said conversationally. "Have a good day?"

Lilah smiled at her, a genuine smile, not the witchy artificial one she always gave me, and the purple light surrounding her body temporarily mellowed to an almost pleasant lavender. "It was pretty good," she said tentatively, and I got the distinct feeling that she was trying not to comment on the fact that I'd lost my lunch in front of the entire high school. I had to give her points for tact.

Lilah turned to look at me. "I'm sorry you puked," she said, sounding like she meant it. "I told Tracy that everyone gets sick and that she'd better not say anything about it. I mean, most of us manage to make it to a trash can before we throw up all over everything, and most of us don't pass out while staring at the math teacher, but still, it's no reason for people to think you're entirely lame."

I took away the points I had given Lilah for tact. It wasn't a quality she possessed in any kind of abundance.

"I brought you your homework," she said, setting it down on the side of my bed. She looked as if she was going to say something else, but instead, she seemed to remember that she was her and that I was me, and that talking to me was not on her priority list of things to be doing with her afternoon.

"Homework on your first day of school?" Lexie asked. "That's unfortunate."

"Is that everything?" I asked, looking at the pile of papers by the side of my bed.

She nodded and arched an eyebrow, looking down at me. "Don't expect me to get your homework tomorrow, though," she said. "I made a vow to never talk to your history teacher again, and that Mr. Kissler gives me the creeps."

I stared at Lilah, completely unaffected by her princess tone or the way that her aura was shifting shades from lavender to a truer purple as she spoke to me. Instead, I thought about how, out of everyone who'd met him, Lilah was the only person so far who didn't think that Mr. Garn was perfection embodied.

Shadows and light.

Great, I thought as the image flashed into my mind. More with the dreams, because what I really needed in the middle of this whole Garn debacle was more confusing dream flashes, like life wasn't cryptic enough already.

Lilah started to walk out of the room, but paused for a

moment. "Later, Lexie," she said. Her eyes flickered to meet mine, and then she turned around and left without so much as a "later" in my general direction.

"Bye," Lexie said. She jabbed me in the side. "Say something," she said quietly.

"Bye," I called weakly, before turning to glare at Lexie. "It wasn't like she said goodbye to me," I told her. "In fact, she very emphatically did not say goodbye to me."

Lexie shrugged. "Does it really matter?" she asked. "I would have said goodbye even if she hadn't said anything to me."

The thing about Lexie was that she was telling the truth. She *would* have.

"Are you connected?" Lexie asked me after a moment. "To Lilah?"

"Very thinly," I said. "You guys are much more connected to each other than she is to me." Looking at Lexie, I was amazed at the sheer number of connective streams that left her aura, making her lights appear as an almost solid cylinder of connections.

"So what are you going to do?" Lexie asked, clearly quelling her urge to grill me more about what I saw of her and Lilah.

That was the question of the moment. There was no way I could sit through class after class and listen to someone who I knew was doing something horrid talk about the x-axis and graphing calculators. Maybe Lexie was right. Maybe I did have some obligation to find out what it was that he was doing and stop it.

Then again, I also had to figure out how to pay attention in all my other classes despite the fact that the thousands of connections I saw all the time were almost blinding; how to redeem myself from Barf Girl status; and, in my spare time, how to use my newfound connection abilities for good, not evil. To top it all off, my thoughts were still jumbled, dreams mixing in with reality, and my mind was still fuzzy. Inside my head, some big piece of the puzzle was missing, and I just couldn't put my finger on it.

I turned to Lexie to answer her question. "I have no idea what I'm going to do," I said, because I really didn't. Not saying another word, I rolled over in bed and reached for my telephone. Even though I knew I wasn't going to be telling him any of this, what I wanted more than anything else in the world was to hear Paul's voice. I dialed the number, and Lexie, taking the hint, slipped out of the room.

No answer. Wherever Paul was, he certainly wasn't sitting at home next to his phone waiting for me to call. Somehow, I wasn't surprised.

Shadows and light.

"And Garn," I added under my breath, but in that instant, the image from the dream was gone. Lying there, I couldn't shake the feeling that Lexie was right. I had to do something, I just had no idea what.

8

midnight

Oklahoma was officially an alien planet. At first, I'd
thought maybe it was just Emory High that was twisted
and bizarre, but one day at home sick had convinced me
otherwise. The whole state was backwards. Not in the
marrying-your-cousin kind of way I'd always thought
Oklahoma was backwards, but as I sat there in my bed,
staring at the television, I was horrified.

"Eight, seven central," I said out loud. I'd heard the
phrase said maybe a million times, but I'd never actually
realized that the "seven central" part meant that, in the
central time zone, television shows came on an hour earlier than they did in normal parts of the country. This
was going to completely throw off my entire TV-
watching schedule.

Forget the facts that Oklahoma actually had some
decent malls, that the carryout my dad had brought
home the day before was to die for, and that the Goldens

were more fashion conscious than just about anyone I'd ever met in California. This whole central-time-zone thing totally put Oklahoma back in the Stone Age or something.

If, you know, they'd had television in the Stone Age.

I sent my television a disgusted look and rolled over onto my side. Something about staying home sick in my new home made me feel like pouting, even though back home, I'd loved to stay in bed all day, knowing that I should be in school, enjoying the way the ocean looked from my bedroom.

From my new window, all I could see was the house across the street.

It could be worse, my inner voice reminded me. *You could be at school right now.*

For once, my conscience and I were totally on the same page. If I thought things had been bad with the Goldens before, I didn't even want to know what it would be like after I'd puked in front of the entire school.

Forget the puking. You should be worrying about Kissler.

Oh yeah. That.

I'd gone to the trouble of convincing my mom to let me take a sick day for the sole purpose of figuring out a plan with regard to Mr. Gloom-and-Doom precalc teacher, but so far, all I had done was yell at my television for the central-time-zone thing.

Glaring at the TV once more for good measure, I hopped off my bed and wandered over to the corner of my room. We hadn't gotten all our furniture situated yet, so my computer was sitting on the floor. Luckily, contrary to what I had previously believed, high-speed Internet had in fact made its way to the middle of the country, and my parents were feeling just guilty enough about moving us to practically the other side of the globe that my dad had connected me first thing yesterday morning.

Sitting on the floor (because, of course, my desk and my chair were still downstairs in the living room where the movers had accidentally left them two days before), I tried to pull myself together and set my hands on the keys. If someone had asked me how I planned to stop a soulless monster from pretending to be a debonair math teacher at a small Oklahoma high school by surfing the Internet, I wouldn't have had a good answer.

Determined to distract myself, I clicked on my IM icon and launched the program. It was nine in the morning in California. With any luck, Paul would be in his computer science class, pining away because I wasn't there to pass notes to, inconspicuously checking his e-mail every few minutes.

As soon as my buddy list popped up, I looked for Paul's screen name, but, alas, it wasn't there, so instead, I opened my Internet browser and checked my e-mail. I raked my eyes over my inbox: something asking me to fill out a survey; something Lexie, queen of the e-mail chain letter, had forwarded me the night before; someone promising to increase my sex drive. . . .

I quickly deleted the spam and scanned the rest of

my new mail. There was nothing, absolutely nothing from Paul.

Frowning at the screen, I impulsively hit the Compose Message button, and before I knew it, my fingers were flying over the keys.

Dear Paul,

Uggggggggg. I sounded completely lame. Backspacing, I tried again.

Hey, Loser. Miss me much? (If the answer's no, just know that I'll be coming to kill you in your sleep as soon as I manage to get away from the alien planet called "Oklahoma" where I'm currently being held hostage.) I miss you tons. The other night was . . . amazing.

Did that sound too desperate? It wasn't exactly a breathy "take me, take me now," but still, for all I knew, Paul thought our kiss had been a mistake, and I'd seen him date enough other girls to know that he so didn't go for the clingy type. Highlighting the last two sentences, I deleted them.

I miss you and Jules tons.

That was far safer. Mentioning Jules, my best girlfriend from home, definitely put less pressure on Paul to talk about the kiss if he didn't want to.

You wouldn't believe this place, Paul. It's insane and not at all like we imagined. You know that time we watched "Carrie" and wondered who in the *world* would pour pig's blood all over someone? Well, I've found the people who do such things. They are evil incarnate. They can smell fear. They are the Goldens (I swear, that's what they call themselves!), and somehow, I managed to offend one of them my first day here by, get this, being hit in the head by a football.

I paused. Would Paul really care about any of this? He'd never even cared about the social scene at our old school, so why would he care about the Golden/Non clique warfare? Typing it out, it all sounded so much more laughable than it felt. Frustrated, I grabbed a ponytail holder off the floor and pulled my hair out of my face.

A blipping sound from my computer made me look up. An instant message from a screen name I didn't recognize stared back at me.

SongCutieGirl: i have decided to forgive u.

I stared at the screen, my mind racing over a possible list of people I knew who would actually pick something like SongCutieGirl for a screen name.

SongCutieGirl: helloooooooo? didn't u hear what i said? i'm going to forgive u.
LissyLou45: Forgive me for what? Who is this?

There was a long pause.

> SongCutieGirl: duh! this is tracy. i'm in study
> hall, and i just wanted u to know, no hard
> feelings about u trying to get in my boyfriend's
> pants.

My mouth actually dropped open.

> SongCutieGirl: because tate's totally not
> interested. i mean, after yesterday, who
> would be, right?

I couldn't even begin to form a coherent response, and in the next instant, I got another instant message.

> MidnightSunshine17: Is Tracy IM-ing you?
> LissyLou45: Yes. Who is this?
> MidnightSunshine17: I told her not to IM you.
> What's she saying?
> LissyLou45: Not much. Who is this?

Conspicuous silence. When a third window popped up, I had a feeling that Tracy wasn't the only one in study hall.

> FuchsiaReynolds: are you feeling better?

At least there was no mystery as to who the third IM-er was, which meant that MidnightSunshine was probably Lilah. And here I'd thought staying home meant I wouldn't have to worry about the three of them.

> FuchsiaReynolds: i thought you should know.
> tracy's been telling everyone your belemic.

It took me a minute to wade through the horrible spelling.

> LissyLou45: Because bulimics often purposefully throw up in front of everyone their first day at a new school.
> FuchsiaReynolds: well . . . are you?

Apparently, sarcasm was totally lost on Fuchsia.

> SongCutieGirl: did u just tell Lilah I was talking to u????
> LissyLou45: Yes.
> SongCutieGirl: well it doesn't even matter anymore, b/c u have been Non-ed. lilah can't help u and tate doesn't want u and I don't even care if u hit on him anymore, cause he'd never date a Non.

My speaker went crazy, blaring out little dings as all three of them IM'd me at once.

> FuchsiaReynolds: you can totally tell me if you are. i won't tell anyone.

MidnightSunshine17: Did you just tell Fuchsia
you were bulimic? Did you give yourself brain
damage yesterday or have you always been an
idiot?
SongCutieGirl: http://IMcentral.org/
userprofiles/FuchsiaReynolds.html

I couldn't help myself. My mind spinning, I clicked
on the link Tracy had sent me, and in the next instant,
Fuchsia's user profile popped up. Fuchsia had cut and
pasted her buddy list into the profile. Sure enough, at the
very bottom, there I was.

I was officially a Non. Or, how had Tracy put it?
I'd been Non-ed. Did this mean they'd leave me
alone now?

Without waiting for another onslaught of IMs, I
quickly closed the window and signed off. At least when I
talked to Lilah and company in person, I could read their
auras and get a feel for what they were thinking. Online
conversations meant no auras, and I just was *not* up to
dealing with the Goldens with one hand tied behind my
back.

My eyes flitted back to my message to Paul. After only
half a day at my new school, I'd managed to have the
loser label slapped on my forehead in what had to be
world-record timing. Moving on impulse, I clicked the
little *X* in the corner of my inbox and closed the e-mail I
was writing.

I flopped onto my bed and hugged a pillow to my chest. To my horror, I could feel tears coming to my eyes.

"This is stupid," I muttered furiously. "I didn't even want to be Golden." Granted, that didn't mean I didn't want them to want me to be Golden, but still. I closed my eyes, trying not to think of the fact that Audra probably would totally disown me as a friend if she knew I was crying over something like this.

The darkness was familiar, the silence grating. Somewhere in my mind, I knew that I'd been here before, knew that I was dreaming, but I couldn't quite force myself to wake up.

Three intertwining circles. The image burned through my mind and through the air, and in the next instant, the space was filled with colored lights: flashing and twisting and turning.

"Where are you?" The words were out of my mouth before I knew that I was asking for the woman who'd entered my dream before: the dark-haired, solemn-eyed woman who had touched my face with her cold, soothing hands.

"Where are you?" a voice repeated.

Whirling around, I found myself staring at Lilah. Her midnight black hair glowed in the aura lights that filled the darkness.

"What are you doing here?" I asked, disgusted.

"What are you doing here?"

The body was Lilah's, but the voice was not.

"Who are you?" My voice shook. "What are you trying to tell me?"

"What are you trying to tell me?" At the sound of another voice, I spun around. Lexie stared back at me, her pixie face clashing with the throaty voice with which she'd spoken.

Three intertwining circles, rings of different colors on a silver shield.

Lexie and Lilah stood next to each other for a moment, their forms blurring and merging and shifting, until another person stood before me.

Me. *"You only see what you want to see,"* the ancient voice with my face said. *"See. Remember. Know."*

Shadows and light. Shadows and light and colors, and then, there was nothing.

"Oh, Katie, this place is absolutely darling!"

I awoke to the distinct sound of moms schmoozing downstairs.

"See, remember, know," I said out loud, shuddering. "See what? Remember what? Know . . ."

"You know, Katie, I can recommend a wonderful cleaning woman. She'd do wonders with this little mess of yours."

Those words, spoken in a clear, high voice, got my attention. If there was one thing my mom hated, it was anyone thinking she was anything less than the perfect housekeeper. Back in California, I'd once seen her dust our plants because she thought they were looking too dirty. People who dusted plants didn't deal well with insinuations that their new houses were an absolutely darling mess.

Curiosity got the better of me, and I tiptoed out of

the room and halfway down the stairs to get a look at the women talking to my mother.

"You always were so creative," a petite blond woman said, and her aura, spindling like crazy, lashed out at my mother's green lights. The scary blond lady, who looked a little Stepford Wives-y to me, arched an eyebrow at the significantly less scary-looking brunette standing beside her. "Do you remember the dress Katie wore to the Senior Gala?" she asked. "It was so daring and creative. It really made a statement."

On the word "statement," the woman's aura jiggled back and forth tauntingly.

"And who is this?" The scary blond lady's words took me by surprise, and I found her eyes directly on mine.

"Lissy," my mom said, and instead of sounding perturbed that I was out of bed when I was supposed to be deathly ill, she sounded almost grateful to see me. Keeping my eyes on the two women, I walked the rest of the way down the stairs to stand next to my mother. My aura, currently a pastel blue, pulled toward hers, the connection between us pulsing as we made eye contact.

"Cindy, Cheryl," my mom said, and the colored lights surrounding her body waved in the aura equivalent of an eye roll. "This is my oldest, Lissy. Lis, Cheryl, Cindy, and I went to high school together when we were your age."

And in that moment, everything became perfectly

clear. Cindy and Cheryl were my mom's Lilah, Tracy, and Fuchsia, and now that she was back in town . . .

"They just dropped by to bring us a housewarming casserole," my mom continued, her teeth gritted.

"Lissy, did anyone ever tell you that you look just like your mother did at your age?" The scary blond lady (I was putting odds down that she was Cheryl) looked me up and down with an appraising eye, and I got the distinct feeling that she wasn't complimenting me.

"Thanks," I said, and Cheryl balked for just a moment.

"It's so refreshing to see a young girl who embraces a natural look," Cheryl continued.

As her aura, a deep, royal purple, mocked me with sharp little waves, I correctly interpreted her words. "Natural look" was Mom Code for no makeup, wearing Snoopy pajama bottoms, and having hair that was so tangled and messy that it looked like it could easily devour the entire state of Oklahoma with its frizziness.

"I was just telling my Fuchsia that the natural look might come back in," Cheryl continued, "but she insists that it's 'so over.'" Cheryl shrugged. "And when it comes to fashion, I have to admit, Fuchsia knows more than I do."

"Fuchsia?" I repeated. The first time she'd said the name, I'd desperately hoped that I was having auditory hallucinations.

"My daughter," Cheryl said. "Do you two know each other?"

As the words left her mouth, I started realizing what exactly it was about this scary blond lady that seemed so familiar. The way she stood, looking down at my mom even though my mom was taller; the way her hair was combed perfectly into place; the way her aura tried to take up the entire room; the way she kept playing nice-nice with her words while the lights around her body tried to devour us whole . . .

Apparently, bitchiness was hereditary.

"Lissy, babe, you don't look like you're feeling that well," my mom said, squeezing my side as our aura connection pulsed again. "Why don't you head back upstairs and I'll bring you some orange juice as soon as Cheryl and Cindy leave?"

As far as subtle hints went, it wasn't exactly subtle. *Chalk one up for Mom,* I thought. Not about to be stuck in the room with Fuchsia's mother for a second longer, I hightailed it back up the stairs, feeling a little guilty about leaving my mom to deal with the Golden Seniors.

She's a big girl, my inner voice said. *She can handle it. Besides, she probably has more dirt on them than they could even imagine. And don't you have some Garn prevention to be working on?*

Not for the first time, I wished that I'd had my mother's Sight instead of my own. To be able to see what people did when they didn't know you were there, to get visions of things that were actually happening. Embarrassing things. Really, truly, horribly embarrassing things.

124

The possibilities for blackmail were almost endless.

"Now, Katie, you absolutely must tell us what is going on with Corey and that Emily Covington."

I glanced back down the stairs over my shoulder as I heard my uncle's name.

"The whole town is just buzzing about the two of them," Cindy piped up. "What with him being a doctor and her being . . ."

Cindy's silence spoke volumes.

"Emily's a doctor too," my mother said bluntly.

"Well, yes," Cheryl sniffed, "and we all admire her for it so much."

Liar, I thought.

"But to think of your baby brother with someone who got into trouble at such a young age . . ."

Trouble? What trouble?

"Trouble?" my mom asked, her voice bordering between skeptical and uninterested. "What trouble?"

Apparently, logic and reason in the face of bitchiness was also hereditary.

"Well, you've met her daughter, haven't you?" Cindy asked, *tsk*ing her tongue. "That poor girl. Imagine growing up with no father and a mother young enough to be your sister."

"And then she *went* to *med school*," Cheryl added, as if going to med school while raising a child was one of the seven deadly sins, right up there next to shooting your neighbor to covet his wife and eating a full box of Krispy Kreme donuts in one sitting.

125

I couldn't take it anymore. My head throbbed, and I walked the rest of the way into my room, closing the door behind me and shutting out the sounds of catty mom chitchat. On my computer screen, there was an instant message waiting for me.

> MidnightSunshine17: I told Fuchsia and Tracy not to say anything else about the bulimia thing. I mean, it's so obvious that you're not. You're not even that skinny! Anyway, just wanted you to know that they'll keep their mouths shut, but if you could stop pissing them off . . . well, let's say it's better to be Non-ed for now than Non-ed for life and I'm getting tired of cleaning up your messes. Ciao.

I didn't care what those women downstairs said, there was no "poor little girl" in this picture. At Emory High, Lilah was queen, or at least, queen enough that even Fuchsia, hereditary bitch, bowed to her superiority. Glaring at the screen, I seethed. Like I'd even asked her to clean up my messes. I didn't *have* any messes, at least not any that didn't involve my Sight and a certain evil math teacher with a pukeworthy aura, and, Golden Queen or not, that was so out of Lilah's domain.

See. Remember. Know.

The words came into my mind without any warning. Calmly, I walked over to my bed, picked up a pillow, put it to my face, and screamed.

Stupid Sight. Stupid Lilah. Stupid eight, seven central. Stupid dreams. Stupid Fuchsia Reynolds, who couldn't even spell "bulimia" right. Stupid Tracy, who thought I was trying to get into her boyfriend's pants. Stupid Goldens. Stupid murderous math teacher.

"This place," I mumbled under my breath in the most brilliant statement I'd made all day, "is stupid."

My computer made a bleeping sound, but instead of reading the instant message that popped up, I flipped off the screen and flopped back onto my bed, stared up at the ceiling, and waited for things to stop sucking.

9

sunset

"And what was the real motivation behind this so-called tea party?" Mr. Wood's aura practically burst in excitement over the Boston Tea Party, but I was too hungry to pay much attention to his answer. It had been two days since I'd looked straight into the black hole of doom that was my supposedly sainted math teacher's soul light, one day since Lilah had told me she was tired of cleaning up my messes, and seventeen minutes since the last time one of the Golden boys in the back row had made not-so-subtle puking sounds in my general direction. My mind was still a mess of garbled images and half-remembered dreams, and so far, the sum total of plans I'd come up with for facing Mr. Kissler included refraining from eating so that I didn't hurl in front of the entire school (again).

On edge, I kept my eyes focused on the occupants of

the classroom, eliminating the chance that I'd somehow catch a glimpse of Mr. Kissler that would send me reflashing back to my first day of school, which I'd christened Barf Day.

Beside me, one of Tate's aura strings wriggled restlessly, and I turned my attention to his lights, because they simultaneously seemed more interesting than the history lecture and felt less apocalypse-y than thinking about the Garn man. Staring at the moving cord of light, I could see it stretching out the door, and I just knew that it was the string that connected him to Tracy.

Without meaning to, I felt myself leave my body, and my ghost self appeared standing beside my desk. I looked down and saw my body still sitting at the desk, an almost tortured look on my face. I waved my ghost hand in front of my real eyes, watching the near transparent outline of a hand move as I did so. Being out of my body felt good. In the ghost body, I didn't feel so hungry, and I didn't have to worry about my stomach churning at the very thought of what was to come.

Testing my balance on my ghost legs, I strolled around the room. Clearly, no one else could see me. As if in a trance, I walked toward Tate and was overcome with an incredible urge to give the wiggling connection a good yank. I might not have been able to do anything about Mr. Kissler, but I could stick it to Tracy right then and there.

No. I stopped myself. I wasn't going to interfere with

129

this. I couldn't go from looking at Garn to doing something like that to someone else, at least not yet. It just didn't feel right. Even in my ghost body, I wasn't really free. The feeling of dread was still there in the corner of my mind, lurking.

Desperate for distraction, I took in the colors of the room: purple, violet, blue, turquoise, yellow, goldenrod, peach, pink, red, fuchsia, sunset orange. Thinking for a moment, I closed my ghost eyes and saw only two colors: turquoise and sunset, and when I opened my eyes again, I looked for the people sporting those colors.

One was a girl to my left who I couldn't remember seeing before. She wasn't pretty in the way that Lilah was pretty, and she wasn't Tracy's bottled blond, but she wasn't unfortunate-looking either. Her aura was bright in color, but small and understated in size.

The boy's aura was the opposite: bigger than it should have been, and not quite a bright enough color for a true turquoise. I walked over to him, noticing the way he was sitting in his desk, relaxed and obviously not paying much attention, his arm dangling casually over the side. He thought he was pretty hot stuff. Looking back at the girl, I wondered why in the world these two had stuck out in my mind so much.

He was definitely a Golden, and she definitely wasn't. Neither of them so much as looked at the other as I stood there in my other-body watching, and yet, looking at their colors, I felt like they belonged together.

What the heck, I thought, waiting for my inner voice to

chime in with a strict warning. Nothing happened, and I took that as permission for what I did next.

Leaning over, I ran my hand through the boy's aura. Like metal shavings to a magnet, his light jumped into my hand in tiny bits, bending his aura to face me a little more. Walking across the room with his aura in my hand, I stretched it and reached out with my other hand to grab a piece of hers. Soon, I held a light string in each hand.

I took a deep breath and knotted them together, waiting. Almost immediately, the strings tried to pull apart, but the action only tightened the knot.

"Are you quite sure you're feeling all right, Miss James?" Mr. Wood asked me, standing right next to the desk and snapping me back into my body. Once I was there, I realized that my physical eyes were closed and that it must have looked an awful lot like I was sleeping. I opened my eyes quickly and looked at the teacher sheepishly.

"I'm fine," I said, for maybe the thousandth time that day. Asking me if I felt all right had become all the rage. Granted, most of the time, there was an unspoken word at the end of the sentence, as in, are you feeling all right today, loser?

Concentrating on staying in my body and not thinking about the fact that I was a mere six hours away from being trapped in a room with Mr. Kissler and the aura of doom and a full seven hours away from escaping the stares of every other student in the school, I spent the rest of the class trying to take notes on the American Revolution and watching the two people I'd tied together.

131

The bell rang, and they both headed for the door. I held back, half because I didn't want to brave the hallway, and half to watch their interaction.

The connection I'd tied vibrated a bit as they headed for the door, and like elastic, it pulled the two of them together, shortening until they were standing right next to each other. With my mouth slightly open, I watched as the two of them actually ran into each other.

Great, I thought dryly, *my attempt at matchmaking ends up in collision. Perfect.*

Both sunset girl and turquoise boy fell to the ground, and for some reason, I pictured them as bowling pins and me as a bowler working on a seven-ten split. I shook my head, disgusted at my own thoughts. For one thing, I was a horrible bowler, and for another, who thought in terms of bowling metaphors anyway? There was no way I could answer that mental question with any mental answer except: a complete reject.

The two of them sat on the ground for a moment, dumbfounded.

Fuchsia, her aura a particularly lethal shade of purpley pink, looked down at them on the floor. "Klutzy much?" she asked the girl, putting a ridiculous amount of valley girl into her voice considering that she was from Oklahoma.

"Come on, Colin," Fuchsia continued, holding out a hand to him and bending down. I could see dozens of little strings extending from her aura, gently brushing up against his in a flirty way. Suddenly, the phrase "hooking a guy" had a totally new meaning.

Turquoise Colin didn't say anything to Fuchsia. His eyes were locked on Miss Sunset's. I smiled to myself.

A swing and a miss, I thought in Fuchsia's general direction. *Take that for putting me on your Non list.*

"Sorry," sunset girl said, looking down and away from Colin. Mentally, I urged her to look up at him. He was staring at her.

"Hey, no problem," he said, smiling.

"Colin," my favorite fuchsia girl said, a little tension entering her too-cheerful voice. "Let's go."

Colin looked at the sunset girl for a little longer. "See you around," he said, pausing then and searching for the girl's name.

Tell him, I told her silently. She, of course, didn't hear me, but in the next second, she obeyed me anyway.

"Sarah," she told him softly.

"Nice to meet you. Charmed, I'm sure," Fuchsia told Sarah quickly and with a bite of sarcasm, a bored expression on her face, and nails in her eyes.

"See you around, Sarah," Colin said softly, looking her directly in the face.

She smiled at him, and the smile made all the difference in the world for her looks. Miss Not-Unfortunate-Looking was actually a cutie underneath the somber expression.

"See you around," she said so softly that I had to read her lips. "Colin," she added more daringly.

I smiled. The seeds of crushdom had been planted, and as they spoke, I could see the rough knot I'd tied

133

between them swirling gently, untying and retying itself in new ways. Success. I'd actually done something, it had actually worked, and I actually felt like smiling again, even though my time was ticking away.

By the time I slipped into a seat at Audra's lunch table, my stomach was killing me and I'd been asked how I was feeling by every person in the entire school. The Barf Girl thing went unstated.

"Feeling well today?" I asked her before anyone could ask me a version of the same question.

Tracy and Tate came into the room. She had her arm wrapped around his waist. He looked slightly uncomfortable with it and very studly in general.

"A bit nauseous," Audra replied levelly, arching one eyebrow a bit as she watched the two of them walk in.

I stifled a grin, and for reasons I couldn't name, as I sat there at the table with her, it was on the tip of my tongue to tell Audra everything: the connection I'd tied that morning, the way Tate was finally slipping away from Tracy, the way I'd been officially declared a Non, and the way I was afraid that precalc was going to end up killing me. Literally.

Dylan plopped down in the seat next to me, and I closed my mouth. What had I been thinking? The Sight was a secret. An übersecret, not the kind of thing you told people you'd known for less than a week. I picked up my fork and played with the mystery meat on my plate. I hadn't wanted to draw attention to myself by visibly skipping lunch, but I knew there wasn't even the smallest chance that I'd be tempted to eat the chunk of processed fat that was today's special.

"Now why did you go and do something like that to yourself?" Audra asked, gesturing to my food.

"Masochist," Dylan mumbled.

"Big word from the one-syllable prairie dog," I retorted, proud of myself for thinking on my feet, but my heart not really in it.

Dylan grinned, his too-long hair falling in his face as it quickly returned to his typical completely blank expression. "What can I say?" he said, his voice low, not making eye contact. "I'm a literary kind of guy."

Audra snorted. "Like you've been to English class any time in the past three years," she said.

He looked up, the hair still covering his eyes to some degree. "And yet I pass again and again," he said, pointing his fork at her with a smirk. "Think on that."

The exchange felt so normal that I found myself relaxing for the first time all day.

I waited for them to continue bantering, but Dylan fell silent as he began demolishing his food with demon-like ferocity and surgical precision.

I looked at my watch. T-minus three hours until my math class.

Audra finally filled the silence. "Huh," she said, chewing her food. I looked at her, again overcome with an urge to blurt out everything. "Sarah Cummings and Colin

Adams," she said. "Major weirdness there. She's sitting at his table, and the Golden girls do not look happy."

Dylan continued staring at his food and completely ignoring the two of us. I wanted to smack him. He was just the kind of guy who irritated me most: quiet and brooding and too shaggy for his own good, and yet, just sitting there, I found myself drawn to his aura. Not wanting to give him any ideas, I tore my eyes away from the light shining out of his face and looked across the lunchroom, praying silently that Mr. Kissler wouldn't make an encore appearance.

After a moment, I let out a breath of relief. No Garn. Instead, I saw Miss Sunset and Mr. Turquoise sitting together. All around them, the purple auras moved in a way that definitely needed a soundtrack composed primarily of hissing and possibly a single inhuman war cry.

I felt myself leaving my body to get a closer look at the connection between the two, but as soon as I saw that it was still holding, I willed myself back into my body. The last thing I wanted was to fall asleep in my uneaten lunch slop.

"Check it out, Lissy," Audra said suddenly. "There's Mr. Kissler. You lost your lunch before you got to observe his hotness before."

"She hasn't eaten any lunch this time," Dylan chimed in. So now Mr. Observant was ready to talk. How peachy.

My heart beating in my ears and my palms sweating, I found myself turning around slowly.

136

Abort mission! Abort mission! my inner voice shouted, seconds too late.

His aura was smaller today, pulled tighter to his body, and there were no connections streaming off it, but that didn't make it any less horrible. Actually, it just made the Garn concentration denser, and I had to bite my tongue to keep myself from giving in to the roaring in my ears. Dylan leaned forward a little bit, and I caught sight of the pearly white light coming out of his face.

Slowly, the nausea and dizziness subsided, and I could feel my tongue throbbing from how hard I had been biting it. I stopped biting it, tasting blood, and looked at Dylan, amazed that his white light had made me feel not so helpless.

At least he was good for something.

From across the cafeteria, Mr. Kissler looked directly at me and smiled. I didn't like that smile, and I did not trust that man. He crossed the cafeteria, walking straight by us and winking at me. Only looking at Dylan's light stopped my hurl reflex.

The math teacher from hell walked up to one of the Golden tables with a smile, and several of the Goldens acknowledged him. I couldn't help but notice the way all the girls' lights perked up when he walked over there, pulling toward him.

Little wires of Garn streamed off his aura, caressing theirs one at a time, and each aura shuddered under his touch. I was torn between wanting to gouge my eyes out and wanting to chuck something at the girls smiling blindly up at him. How could they not feel what he was? Were they that disconnected from their auras?

"Are you okay?" Audra asked me. "You look kind of pale."

Dylan didn't say anything, but he looked at me carefully. I couldn't read the expression in his eyes, and his white light wasn't giving me any clues as to what he was thinking.

Three intertwining circles, rings of different colors on a silver shield.

The moment after the image hopped into my mind, it was gone. I still had no idea what to do about Mr. Kissler and a feeling in the pit of my stomach that I needed to figure it out, quick.

I hadn't asked for this responsibility. It was my second day at a new school, and all I really wanted was something to eat, but I had the distinct feeling that eating the food I'd bought would be a sure recipe for an encore Barf Girl performance.

The Garn streams recoiled into Mr. Kissler's aura with a snap, and even holding Dylan's aura in my gaze, I winced. No matter how hard I tried, even being in the room with that much Garn hurt my eyes and my heart, and I couldn't shake the feeling that there was something I was supposed to be remembering that was just out of reach.

10

green

Just when I was thinking that life could not possibly take another turn toward the strange, it did.

"Are you a soprano?" Miss Cutler, the peppy young music teacher, asked me. She was a bright green, and looking at her gave me a slight headache, especially since she was absolutely connection happy, with little green strings streaming off her body in all directions, and it was hard for me to even look at connections without reflashing to the way the other auras had shuddered under Kissler's touch. "You look like a soprano."

"I don't sing," I replied flatly, forcing myself back to the present.

She laughed, gratingly musical laughter. "Don't be ridiculous," she said. "Everyone can sing."

I didn't say anything, but as I crossed my arms over my chest, I knew that one chorus teacher was about to be snapped out of her theoretical world to my unfortunately real one. I didn't even sing "Happy Birthday" at parties. That's how bad I was, and yet, someone had seen fit to sign me up for chorus. I made a mental note to find out who exactly had picked out my classes for this school year. Whoever it was needed to suffer as I was suffering.

I waited, knowing that Miss Cutler was going to ask me to sing for her. She did. I considered staunchly refusing, but since I knew from experience that I wasn't very good about being staunch, I just went along with this new and unique form of humiliation.

"Can you believe her?" a voice rang out behind me. I knew without looking that it was Tracy, and I ignored her, even though I knew there was a good chance she was talking about me. With my luck, she'd probably thought of a brand-new rumor to start about how I'd tried to seduce her boyfriend with my sensual barfing skills. I shuddered at the thought of it.

"Let me hear an A," Miss Cutler said.

"A whosit?" I asked, staring at her blankly.

She was quiet for a moment, trying to figure out what in the world I was trying to say. My clueless expression tipped her off.

"Oh dear," she said. "You don't know music notes?"

I shook my head. "It wouldn't matter if I did," I said. "I'm tone deaf. It all sounds the same." That wasn't quite true, but I didn't want to give the poor woman any false hope. There was no world in which I could sing. I knew my own limitations, and they definitely laid the smack-down whenever I tried to make any sound remotely musical.

Miss Cutler opened her mouth and let out a high and clear note. "Try that," she said.

Look, lady, I thought, *you do not want to hear me sing. Just trust me on this one.*

Of course, I didn't actually say that out loud. My limitations wouldn't let me. The only adult I could ever actually talk to that bluntly was my uncle Corey, and after the past couple of days, I didn't think I'd be talking to the Emily-fied version of Corey the same way from now on.

"I'll try," I sighed.

You'll be sorry, I thought to her silently.

You will be too, my inner voice told me, finally taking a break from singing the single note of dread that had filled my mind all day.

I ignored it and opened my mouth to air-quote sing.

"Well then," Miss Cutler said, clearly at a loss for words. She paused and clasped her hands together. "I think you're an alto," she said brightly.

Uh-huh, I thought. That was definitely not what she was thinking. Her green aura flashed like a strobe light as she tried to smile cheerfully at me.

"Why don't you go stand by Lilah?" she asked, gesturing with her arms. "She's the one in the lovely white tank."

"I know who she is," I said, putting the same fake cheerfulness into my voice that she had in hers. I could never keep my voice from badly mimicking those around me; as it was, I was beginning to pick up a very fake-sounding Oklahoma accent. Sooner or later, someone was going to get insulted, but I had enough things to deal with without worrying about that.

"Of course you know Lilah. You're Corey Nowly's niece," Miss Cutler remembered. "How silly of me." Apparently, the entire town knew about my uncle and Lilah's mom, which made sense. Fuchsia's mom had acted like it was front-page material, and everyone seemed to know that the only reason Lilah tolerated me at all was that my uncle was dating her mom. In my opinion, everyone in this town knew way, way too much, except for when it came to homicidal math teachers, and then they knew way, way too little.

Shadows and light.

As I moved toward Lilah and Tracy and tried to sort through the jumble of memories flashing through my mind, I knew I was a dead girl walking. I couldn't help but wonder how I'd managed to end up in so many classes with girls a year older than I was. The advanced classes I understood, but chorus? The schedule gods were clearly spiting me.

"I mean, honestly, like she even stands a chance with Colin," Tracy said, shooting darts at me out of the corner of her eye. It took me a second to figure out that for once she wasn't talking about me.

142

"He probably just thinks she's easy," Fuchsia sniffed.

I stifled a snort. Fuchsia was falling out of her shirt, so, of course, the logical thing to assume about poor conservatively dressed Sunset Sarah was that she was easy. I just loved the way these girls' minds worked. Suddenly, the barf seductress rumor scenario wasn't looking so far-fetched.

"Don't worry, Fuchsia," Lilah said, speaking for the first time. "There won't be anything there." Lilah said the words with absolute confidence. Of course, if the queen had declared it to be true, it would be true, sunset and turquoise be damned.

"Oh," Lilah said, seeing me approach and sounding less than thrilled about it. "Hi." She didn't say anything else. I was a little surprised that she had said anything at all.

"So what do you think, Lissy?" Tracy asked, tilting her head to the side. Her voice sounded pleasant, but small pieces of her aura were jutting in and out at odd angles, in the same sort of hissing dance the Goldens' auras had performed during Sarah's invasion of their sacred lunch space.

"About what?" I asked innocently, trying to avoid a bullet by not answering the question and resisting the reflash that desperately wanted to come.

"Nothing," Lilah said quickly. Tracy wasn't to be dissuaded, probably at least in part because on the boy side of the risers, Tate and Brock were standing together with Colin and another guy I didn't recognize except for recognizing his confident stance and overgelled hair as indicators of his Golden status. Tracy wasn't about to let me off easy with Tate's presence just out of earshot reminding her that she hated me for no reason at all.

"About the way Sarah Cummings is throwing herself at Colin," Tracy replied. I was very glad for Sarah's sake that she wasn't in this class. What had I started?

Don't be such a wimp, my inner voice said. *They're good together, the turquoise and the sunset. If these girls don't like it, then that's just too bad for them. You don't form the attraction, you just tie the knots and help them along a little. At least you're doing something.*

Knot Tyer wasn't really the title I had been hoping for, and the subtle jab at the fact that I wasn't doing anything where Kissler was concerned wasn't lost on me.

Realizing that the popular girls were all staring at me, I scrambled for an answer. "I don't really know what you're talking about," I said. "Who's Colin? I think Sarah's in my chemistry class, but I'm not sure."

Fuchsia snorted. "Like anyone would know who Sarah was and not Colin. Puh-lease."

"She's only been here for a couple of days," Lilah said in my defense. I couldn't believe she was standing up for me. "And why would she be paying attention to Golden guys anyway? Maybe she just knows her own limitations and doesn't bother to think about them or something. Cut her some slack."

As usual, Lilah managed to insult me when she was trying to be nice. Either that, or she managed to

144

somehow come off as trying to be nice while she insulted me. I wasn't sure which one, and thinking about it gave me as much of a headache as Miss Cutler's strobing green aura did.

From two rows down and halfway across the risers, Audra waved to me, a wicked grin in her eyes. She was enjoying seeing them put me through this. I decided to wait until later to let her know just what I thought about that. I tried to match her smile with a smirk of my own, but I couldn't quite pull it off with Tracy's aura still hissing at me in its own pretty purple way.

As Miss Cutler started taking the group through warm-up exercises, which I mouthed, conversation subsided. The risers were arranged to form half of a six-agon (I could never remember whether it was supposed to be a hexagon or a heptagon). The structure of the risers made it a lot easier for me to examine the connections between people, and while I was busy pretending to sing, I took advantage of that fact in order to try to sort things out a little.

Lilah and Brock were pretty firmly connected with a comfortable knot, but the strings themselves looked tiny today. I wondered why, but couldn't think of a logical explanation. Even as we sang, the knot tying Tate's string to Tracy's was coming undone. Finally. Golden yellow and purple just did not go together, especially this particular yellow and purple pair. He was way too good for her.

Musing, I wondered who would have made a good

match for Tate. He seemed like a nice enough guy, Tracy relationship aside. Golden yellow with orange, maybe? Or were those colors too similar?

"Okay," Miss Cutler said, noticing my waning attention and not really caring just so long as I wasn't singing out loud. "Tracy, you want to start us off with your 'Higher' solo?"

I'd never heard of the song, not that it made a difference. Tracy nodded. It figured that she had the solo, even though it surprised me a little that Lilah didn't have it. Lilah had perfectly straight, gorgeous dark hair, so in my mind, it was only logical that she should be able to sing beautifully.

Tracy opened her mouth, and I noticed that she stared straight at Tate as she sang. "I was lonely and alone, freezing and far too cold, low and getting lower . . ." Tracy's voice was high and rich, and she sang the lyrics with a calmness that surprised me. As she sang, her aura rippled toward the center, purple color gathering tightly near her heart, and as she stared at Tate, his aura pulled toward her.

Gathering into a massive string, her aura snaked out, entwining itself with Tate's until it had a firm grip on his entire being. Tate smiled back at her, and Tracy continued singing. "Then you came, and you lifted me. Higher." Her last note held in the air, and she didn't blink, holding her gaze on Tate as the sound of her voice echoed around the room.

When the entire choir joined in on the song, Tracy's

aura slowly eased its hold on Tate, and she stopped staring at him, a satisfied smile crossing her face. Entranced, I watched as the purple light pulled back to Tracy's body, but not before the string that connected her to Tate was looped about several times, securing the knot.

Well, I thought, *this is certainly an interesting turn of events.*

I stared at Tate's aura openmouthed, all thoughts of Kissler flying out of my mind.

How in the world had Tracy done that? I wasn't even really sure what she had done. Across the room, Tate was gazing at her with an adoring expression on his face. And I had thought Garn was unappetizing.

Wanting a closer look, I let myself slip out of my body. Floating across the room on my ghost legs, which were depressingly more coordinated than my normal legs, I approached the knot that tied the two Goldens together. Tracy's purple was wrapped firmly around Tate's, tied so tightly that the golden yellow string bulged on either side of the knot.

I reached out with my ghost hand to touch the connection, but I paused before I made it as far as pseudo-physical contact. Even just holding my hand over the knot, I felt my fingers starting to sizzle with some kind of unearthly heat. Startled, I yanked my hand away from the aura-slash-string-of-liquid-purple-magma, and the movement flung me back into my real body with a force that caused me to promptly fall off the back of the risers.

My fall was accompanied by a lovely crashing sound that drew everyone's attention directly to me.

Great. That was exactly what I needed after the Barf Girl incident, another reason for everyone to think I was entirely strange. Then again, considering that I'd just had my third or fourth out-of-body experience of the week, I had to admit there was a chance that I had reached bona fide freakhood. Trying not to draw any more attention to myself, I scrambled coolly back onto the risers and avoided all eye contact.

After staring at me for a moment, Miss Cutler clapped her hands sharply. "From the second verse," she said. I was grateful that I didn't have to watch Tracy's aura reprise its role as a romantic lasso. How in the world had she managed that? I couldn't think of a single logical explanation. Instead, I thought of approximately eighteen reasons why I wished I was back in my relatively Garn-free California high school.

At the same time, I kept a close eye on Tracy's aura, but it behaved itself, and nothing else strange happened. As soon as class was over, Tracy sauntered over to Tate. He wrapped his arm around her, and, flashing me a triumphant look, Tracy led him out of the room.

Tate ran into me on the way out, but didn't so much as pause to say he was sorry, let alone look twice in my direction.

"I don't know how she does it," Audra said, coming up beside me with a sigh. "At this rate, they'll never break up. Forget it. I don't want him, not if he's that dumb."

Audra shrugged mid-rant, one of those I've-said-too-much realizations spreading across her face. "I just don't get it," she muttered.

"What's to get?" Fuchsia asked, walking by and overhearing part of our conversation. She leaned in to smile at both of us in a way that made me feel about two inches tall. "She's Golden. You're not."

With that, the girl who was quickly convincing me that fuchsia was a worse aura color than purple was out the door, Lilah walking gracefully at her heels, Brock a step behind them.

"This place is so weird," I muttered, and I wasn't talking about the Garn-covered math teachers or the singing seductress girls. The fact that the popular kids were so well defined freaked me out. At this school, you either were or you weren't, and no one had the least bit of trouble pointing it out to you if you weren't. In fact, they had lists published online. They had a word for what it meant to be declared a loser. I mean, honestly, "Non-ed" . . . what kind of verb was that? What kind of place was this anyway?

I realized then that Audra was waiting for my answer. "I don't know how Tracy does it either," I said, my voice coming out incredibly puzzled. Audra laughed then, shaking it off.

"It's not the Bermuda Triangle, Lissy," she told me, "I guess it's just one of those little high school mysteries we'll never know the answer to."

Hearing Audra say that made me realize that I really

wanted to unravel this mystery, no string-connection pun intended. So far, I didn't know much, just that Dylan, in all his broody-boy wonder, had been wrong. Tracy's hold over Tate had a lot less to do with her chest than it had to do with her voice. Come to think of it, their connection had tightened when even a musical lilt had entered her voice the day I'd thrown up. Whatever was going on, I added it to my long list of things to figure out.

I looked at my watch. T-minus one hour until precalc. I turned to Audra and tried to make my voice sound casual. "Dylan going to math today?" I asked, thinking about the fact that I didn't really want to know what would happen if I was forced to spend an hour in a room with that man without some form of happy pearl Garn shield at my side. I didn't even know for sure that Dylan's aura had made things better. Maybe it had just been my imagination, but I was willing to let my psychosis stay right in place if that was the case.

"I'm not his keeper," Audra said, arching one eyebrow. "But if I had to take a guess, I'd say yes. He's not big on English, but good old Dylan has a thing for math." She paused for a minute and wrinkled her forehead. "Do you have a thing for him?" she asked finally.

I shook my head so quickly that a wayward piece of frizzy hair flew into my mouth. After choking on it for a second, I pried the chunk of hair from my lips, trying not to lose my cool. Not that I'd ever had my cool in the first place.

"No," I said dryly. "A world of no. A gallon of no. An Olympic-sized training pool of no."

Audra grinned. "You have a thing for him," she said, grinning.

I gave her a disgruntled look. "I definitely don't. Trust me, I don't go for broody and shaggy. I'm more of a clean-cut and yet still ruggedly handsome type girl myself."

"That's funny," Audra teased, tweaking my hair. "I never would have pegged you for ruggedly handsome."

"Not me," I muttered, knowing she was teasing, "the guys I like."

"So who do you like?" she asked me. I had the distinct feeling that she was waiting for me to say Tate, but after seeing the way Tracy's purple light had taken over his aura, the last thing I wanted was a piece of that boy. He was like a sick little puppy on a purple aura leash. That was a major turnoff.

"No one here," I said. "There's this guy at home, California home . . ." I trailed off. There wasn't much I could say about Paul, especially since he had yet to return a single one of my phone calls and I'd chickened out of sending him every e-mail I'd tried to write. That little weasel had kissed me, and now he was completely avoiding me.

I looked at my watch again. "We're going to be late," I said, darting into my English class to avoid further questioning and to think for a while on questions of my own. After all, I certainly wasn't going to be thinking about anything even remotely related to the English language or symbolism in the book that I was supposed to have read but hadn't yet. I was anti-simpering, and I knew just from looking at the cover of the book that it was the kind of book in which at least three women were going to simper.

I looked at my watch. T-minus fifty-eight minutes until math.

11

pink

I stood perfectly still, looking at the door to room 106. I reached my hand out to the doorknob and paused for a second. This so wasn't something I wanted to be doing, but then again, my stellar plan of hiding in the girls' bathroom for the entire period was bound for failure from the moment of conception, half because reading what the Golden girls had written on the bathroom stalls about Sunset Sarah was almost as bad as looking into a Garn-colored aura, and half because I didn't want to think of facing my mom and dad if I was caught skipping class on my second day of school, especially since my mom didn't trust my Sight and my dad was totally anti-Sight at the moment.

"What are you doing—walking the plank?" an expressionless voice said from behind me. I whipped around, with every intention of scowling at Dylan, but he was already scowling at me, and that took the wind out of my sails a little.

"I'm not a big fan of math," I said not too smoothly. I was lying, but it wasn't as if I was even thinking about telling him the truth. I wasn't that crazy. I'd never told anyone about my Sight, and I fully intended to keep it that way.

"Whatever," Dylan said, his scowl giving way to smirkville as he leaned in front of me and opened the door.

For some reason, I found myself grinning at him. There was something comical in his motion, and if I hadn't been so on edge, I might have laughed. "After you, matey," I joked, completely in denial about what was about to happen.

He stared at me.

"Pirates," I said simply in explanation.

After a long pause, he grinned. "Yeah," he said. I had a feeling that was as close to a laugh as I was going to be able to get out of him.

Mr. Kissler was standing at the front of the room, writing on the chalkboard. I bit the inside of my lip as I steeled myself against the sickening emptiness of his aura. From a back view, it wasn't that bad, but I shoved Dylan in front of me anyway, twisting him sideways so that I could still see the pearl light coming out of the front of his face.

"Strange," he commented.

"Shut up and walk," I hissed. Surprisingly, he walked sideways down the aisle, earning him some eye-rolling from the group of Goldens concentrated at the front of the room.

"Freak," I heard one of the guys mutter, and I looked in the direction of the voice. So far, I'd had minimal problems with the Golden guys except for the anonymous one who'd been making barfing noises at me in history class. I had even started thinking that, for the most part, it was just the girls who were seriously unhinged, but the voice insulting Dylan was distinctly male. Seeking out the voice's owner, I was surprised to find that I was looking directly at Brock, his blue aura pulled tight to his face. So far, he'd seemed like a pretty decent guy to me, but the way he was smirking at Dylan made me think that maybe he and Lilah deserved each other after all.

I sat down carefully in my seat, trying not to look directly at the teacher. I shoved Dylan into the seat next to me and decided that I could get used to pushing him around. His bad-moodiness wasn't nearly so irritating when I was causing it on purpose.

"Homework check," Mr. Kissler announced as soon as the bell rang. The class let out a collective groan, but there didn't seem to be much heat behind it. I reached into my bag and pulled out the problems Lilah had told me had been assigned. As Mr. Kissler walked around the room, I stared at my paper so hard that the numbers blurred on the page and my eyes teared up. As long as I was looking at the paper, I wasn't looking at him, and the less I looked directly at him, the better.

"Hey there, stranger," a deep and mesmerizing voice said from beside me. "My incredibly developed psychic abilities tell me that you are Lissy James. I'd ask you if you were feeling better, but I'm willing to wager you've been asked that a few too many times today." Listening to him, I almost liked him, but my mind's eye reminded me that if I so much as turned my head, I would discover that I was so close to his aura that it was practically touching me. Even the thought made my stomach turn.

What in the world had he done? What in the world was he doing?

"All right, Lis," he said, "let me take a look at that assignment of yours." I didn't say anything about the way he'd shortened my name in a really familiar way. I could feel the blood starting to run inside my mouth as I bit my lip, careful not to look directly at him as he bent down to my desk. Still, his aura came into my line of vision, and there was no way that I could look away from it without closing my eyes. My heart racing, I realized that Mr. Kissler was standing directly between me and Dylan, so that safety precaution wasn't really an option.

"Looks good." Mr. Kissler nodded. "Welcome to my class, Felicity Shannon James." His voice held on my middle name for the smallest moment, so small that I thought I might have imagined it.

I held my breath, and if the math teacher thought I was acting strange, he didn't say anything as he moved on to the person in front of me. Feeling like I was drowning and desperate for breath, I turned to look at Dylan. He had his head turned in the other direction, and I couldn't see his pearl-colored lights. Without thinking about it, I reached across the aisle and smacked him upside the head. It felt good.

He turned to glare at me. Apparently, it hadn't felt quite so good to him. I ignored his glare, because looking at his aura settled my stomach.

"You've almost got it, Trace," I heard Mr. Kissler saying, "but I think you might need just a little bit of one-on-one attention." His voice sounded almost flirty. Dylan's eyes twitched just a little bit in a motion I equated with an eye roll.

Braving a glance in Tracy's direction, I wondered just how it was that I'd been lucky enough to get in so many of the same classes as the high school's favorite Aura Lassoer. Since Tate wasn't in this class, I didn't have to bother to look at that connection, but Tracy's purple lights were going crazy with Mr. Kissler in close proximity, dancing around him. She was practically drooling, and I half expected her to break into song and wrap a string around the math teacher. It would all have been disturbing sans the fact that I couldn't look directly at Mr. Kissler because of the Garn factor. Somehow, I wasn't surprised that the supreme witch and Mr. Evil got along so well.

I shook my head. There it was again. The feeling that I was missing something, some piece of my memory about what had happened during my first day of school. What was it?

"I'd love some after-school help," Tracy said.

"Tomorrow," Mr. Kissler offered.

"Does that offer extend to everyone?" another girl asked, batting her eyelashes. Tracy shot her a death look.

"Of course," Mr. Kissler said smoothly, "but you're doing just fine, Anna. If you feel you need some extra help, just let me know, and we'll schedule something." With that, he walked to the front of the classroom and began talking in that hypnotically pleasing voice about variables and derivatives, drawing on the board as he did. I stared down at my paper, thinking that I stood absolutely no chance of passing this class. I couldn't very well look at the board without overdosing on Garn, and trying to take notes based on a few charismatic mutterings about numbers and variables wasn't exactly a picnic.

When the bell rang, I darted out of the room before anyone had a chance to say anything to me. As I rounded the corner of the hallway, I found myself not moving anymore. Turning around, I looked at Dylan, who had a firm hold on my backpack. Reaching up carefully and deliberately with the other hand, he smacked me upside the head gently, just enough to irritate me.

"Oh yeah," I said, "that."

"That," he confirmed.

"Sorry?" I said, shrugging. His hair fell into his eyes, and I wondered if I would ever have the opportunity to get close to him with a pair of scissors.

"Why?" he asked simply.

"The ever-present question, my lad," a familiar voice boomed from behind me. "Perhaps you should be asking yourself why *not*." She turned her attention to me. "Don't you have any greeting for an old woman, Lissy of the forest?"

So now I was of the forest. How interesting, and mortifying. Beside me, Dylan's facial expression hadn't changed at all, but I still got the feeling that he was laughing at me inside. My fingers itched to smack him again.

"Hi, Grams," I said, and suddenly, I had a much higher priority on my list of things to do than worrying about Mr. Kissler's sordid past or Tracy's freaky singing trick. The last thing I needed was for Grams to make a scene at my school, and she really couldn't go anywhere without making a scene. I took in her choice of clothing. I wondered who her muumuu supplier was, and made a mental note to make that person suffer immeasurable harm.

"Introduce!" she barked, and as always, I immediately jumped to obey her one-word command.

"Dylan, this is my grandmother. Grams, this is Dylan," I said quickly.

"We've met before," Dylan said dryly.

"Of course we have," Grams said. "This is a small town, boy. Do you fancy my granddaughter?" She didn't so much as pause.

Dylan didn't have anything to say to that, and I practically dragged Grams away from him.

"Lilah," she barked out, passing my favorite purple princess in the hallway, and Lilah, not looking quite as mortified as I felt, followed us silently. It wasn't until I reached the car that I realized Dylan was still with me.

"Answer," he told me, smirking at his own one-word command. I knew he was referring to his question about what had happened in class.

"It doesn't work when you do it," I told him, rolling my eyes.

"Car," Grams said, and Lilah and I jumped. Grams turned her attention to Dylan and gestured to the car, not even bothering to repeat herself. He climbed in, the smirk never leaving his face.

"Hi," Lexie said brightly from the front seat. She turned around and looked at the three of us, squeezed into the tiny backseat of Grams' car. She zeroed in on Dylan in record time. "Who are you? I'm Lexie, Lissy's younger sister. You're an only child, aren't you?"

I had no idea where she was getting these questions from, and Dylan stared at her, a little overwhelmed.

"Seat belts," Grams said, hopping into the driver's seat of her sports car.

Immediately, everyone else went to buckle their seat

belts, and, crammed into the tiny middle seat, I fished around for mine.

"Yeah," Dylan replied, and I couldn't for the life of me remember what question Lexie had asked him.

"You just look like an only child," Lexie told him, no malice in her voice. I grinned. My little sister sounded perfectly sweet, but beside me, Dylan was trying to decide whether or not he had been insulted.

"Do I look like an only child?" Lilah asked from my left. She moved toward the window a little, clearly no more thrilled about the fact that I was practically sitting in her lap than I was.

Lexie thought about it for a minute. "Not quite so much," she replied finally, "but I can still see it."

Lilah wasn't quite sure what to think about that answer, and honestly, neither was I.

"So, you survived today, Lis?" Lexie asked me. From the driver's seat, Grams snorted indelicately and loudly.

"I survived," I said, wanting to tell Lex exactly what had happened in chorus, but knowing that now was not the time. Grams hadn't believed me about Mr. Kissler, so as far as I was concerned, she could suffer with being completely out of the Aura Seer loop, and the last thing Lilah needed to know about me was the fact that I'd been given the gift of enhanced Sight through my bloodlines. Ditto for Dylan.

"I told you that you would be okay," Lexie said, turning on the radio and humming under her breath.

For a while, the five of us rode in silence, and Lilah glanced at Dylan at odd intervals, wrinkling her perfect little nose in a way that so wasn't as subtle as she thought it was.

Pulling into Lilah's driveway, Grams stopped the car and unlocked it. A nanosecond later, Lilah and her back-pack were out of the car and bolting toward her front door.

"Come by and see me, Lilah child," Grams instructed the girl. From the backseat, I snorted. Like that was ever going to happen. Grams turned around and shot me a disgruntled look as she backed out of the driveway.

"You, boy," she said to Dylan.

He was looking out the window and snapped to attention when she spoke to him. I grinned. Seeing Mr. No-Eye-Contact look at Grams as soon as she said a word amused me.

"You'll stay for dinner," Grams said firmly, leaving no room for Dylan to decline the invitation and no room for me to disinvite him. My almighty grandmother had spoken, and so it was going to be.

Grams pulled up to our house. Lexie, Dylan, and I all got out of the car, and a moment later, my grandmother sped out of the driveway.

"Is she going to be at dinner?" Dylan asked, a little awed.

"Who knows?" I said, shrugging.

"She'll know if you aren't there either way," Lexie

pointed out cheerfully. Then she turned to me. "How was Mr. Garn today?" she asked without preamble.

I eyed my little sister. I so wasn't about to talk about this right now. We didn't talk about our gifts with anyone outside the family, and of the many things I already knew Dylan was, gorgeous aura aside, he most definitely was not a member of my family.

Instead of answering, I opened the front door and walked inside. To my relief, no one was home. The last thing I wanted was to introduce Dylan to my parents. For one thing, I wasn't even sure that the two of us were really friends yet, and for another, it would have been just my luck for my mom to make another Paul comment.

"Come on, Lis," Lexie said, ignoring the warning look I was giving her. "What happened during math class? You obviously didn't throw up again. What did you see?"

Dylan crossed his arms over his chest. I could tell just from looking at him that he was very pleased with the direction my little sister's line of questioning was taking.

"I don't want to talk about it now," I said.

"Don't care," Dylan replied, keeping the number of words he was speaking to a minimum.

"It's okay to talk about it around him," Lexie said confidently. As if there was any way she could possibly know that.

"Talk about what?" Dylan asked.

"Nothing," I replied.

"Her Sight," Lexie replied, grabbing a cookie from the jar on the counter and offering one to Dylan. Since when did we have a cookie jar anyway?

"Lex, can I talk to you in the other room?" I asked, fully prepared to give my sister a good maiming once we got there. Lexie grinned at me, and shook her head.

"What Sight?" Dylan asked, sounding interested despite himself.

Lexie gave me a charming look that very clearly told me that if I didn't tell him, she would. I wondered why she was so dead set on my cluing Dylan in. It wasn't like her.

"You aren't going to believe any of it," I told Dylan.

"Yes he will," Lexie said, taking another bite of her cookie.

"Good cookie," Dylan told Lexie, completely ignoring me. He was being about as friendly as I had ever seen him, but most people couldn't help but be friendly around Lexie. She just brought that out in people.

"Fine," I muttered, grabbing a cookie of my own and sitting down at the kitchen table, "but when he thinks we're crazy, I'm going to blame you." I told my sister. She shrugged.

"Whatever," she said around a mouthful of chocolate chips.

I nibbled on the edge of my cookie. "I see auras," I said bluntly.

Dylan stared at me, his facial expression not changing at all as he leaned over to pick up another cookie.

"See?" I told Lexie, crossing my arms over my chest. "He doesn't believe me, he thinks we're both crazy, and he's eating all our cookies."

"Tell him about the math teacher," Lexie said. I refused, and in the next moment, the story began flowing out of Lexie's mouth. "Lissy's always been able to see these colored lights around people. It's her Sight. Everyone in our family has the Sight, the girls at least." She paused for a moment and then continued on quickly. "Anyway, Lissy can tell what kinds of moods people are in when the auras move, and she can tell other stuff too. The thing is, there are as many different aura colors as you can imagine, and there aren't really any bad colors. They're just all different."

I begged to differ on that front. Purple was definitely a bad aura color. I didn't say anything out loud, mostly because Lexie was talking too quickly for me to get a word in edgewise.

"But there's this one color that isn't really a color. I guess it looks like more of a lack of color, and it only appears in someone's aura when they've done something really awful, like kill someone or something. Lissy calls it Garn."

"Nice name," Dylan said, speaking for the first time and interrupting Lexie's speech. She grinned at him, completely unabashed, and continued.

"Anyway, usually even people who have done these

165

incredibly horrible things only have a streak of Garn in their auras, but Lissy's math teacher has an aura that is entirely Garn. She can't even look at it without throwing up and passing out and stuff. That's how incredibly awful it is. Anyway, she needs to find out what he's doing that is so bad, but she has no idea how, and I don't even know how she survived the day at school with Mr. Garn for precalc." Lexie stopped talking and took another bite of cookie, looking quite satisfied with herself for spilling pretty much all the family secrets to a complete stranger.

"So Kissler is Garn," Dylan commented thoughtfully. "I always knew that guy was a sleaze."

I stared at him, completely not believing that his only comment was some teenage boy insult aimed at Mr. Kissler.

"That's it?" I asked him. "She tells you all that, and all you have to say is that Mr. Kissler is a sleaze?"

He shrugged and helped himself to a third cookie. "I have a very open mind," he said wryly. I stared at him. Today was just getting stranger and stranger.

"So you believe it?" I asked him. "About my aura vision and Mr. Kissler being evil and whatnot?"

"That's a pretty big whatnot," he told me, smirking, "but yeah, I do believe it. Somehow, when your sister says all that, I know that it's true."

I looked at Lexie: Miss Credibility. "You wouldn't have believed me," I grumbled.

"No," he agreed. "Probably not. So what did Kissler do that's so awful?"

"That's the question of the day," I said.

"What's the question of the day?" my mom asked, coming into the room.

I smiled up at her. "Nothing," I said. Feeling the awkward silence that followed, I introduced Dylan. "Grams invited him to stay for dinner," I said, letting my mom know exactly what I thought about that. Between my grandmother and my little sister, Dylan was getting the inside track in the getting-to-know-Lissy program. It was just my luck that it was him. I do my civic Aura Seer duty by magically fixing cute Colin up with Sarah the Non, and what do I get in return? Dylan. Life was so not fair.

"Come on," I told Dylan, knowing Lexie would follow. "We'll go up to my room."

My mom smiled at me, a knowing smile that told me she really didn't know anything at all, because she clearly thought that I was romantically interested in Dylan. For someone with the Sight, my mom was so incredibly clueless sometimes, and not in an endearing Alicia Silverstone kind of way, either.

"I'll call up when dinner's ready," my mom told us as we left the room. Dylan and Lexie followed me up two flights of stairs and into my room.

Lexie flopped down comfortably on my bed. "So what else happened today?"

"There's more?" Dylan asked, raising his eyebrows slightly, his hair falling into his face.

"Well," I said, "that was it on the Garn front, but in an interesting sidebar, I tried out tying a connection on my own, and it worked wonders. Oh, and one of the Goldens pulled some sort of singing voodoo on her boyfriend to get him all nice and tied up connection-wise."

Dylan stared at me, a blank expression on his face. I allowed Lexie to explain my newly developed power to see connections and to make or break them as I saw fit.

"You actually do that?" he asked me. "Play with people's lives that way?" He managed to sound disgusted even though there was no tone at all in his voice.

"Hey," I said defensively. "I've only done it once and I just helped some people along a little. I wouldn't break connections, even if I thought things are totally wrong, and I can't make friendship connections. Those are seamless. I can just tie two aura strings together if I think two people would be good together."

"If she's wrong the strings wouldn't stay tied anyway," Lexie said.

"Colin and Sarah," Dylan said, no question in his voice.

I nodded. "Maybe," I said in a tiny voice.

"This is messed up," he told me.

"I'm not hurting anything," I retorted. "You're the one who wanted to hear about it."

"What about the singing girl?" Lexie asked.

"And what was with the way you were looking at me in math class?" Dylan asked, suddenly Mr. Talkative. I sighed and sat down on the floor, letting my head bang against the side of my mattress.

All of a sudden, I had a lot of explaining to do.

12

pearl again

"So how about I go out on a limb here and suggest that we make the Kissler mystery our top priority," said Dylan, relishing his surprise role as Mr. Articulate. "Because I really don't care what goes on in the sordid love lives of people who enjoy making my life miserable, and call me old-fashioned, but supernatural matchmaking isn't really my thing."

I narrowed my eyes at him. I'd liked him better before he'd started using complex sentences.

"But what can we do?" Lexie asked, her face practically pink with excitement and her aura increasing in size by the second. It was easy for me to see that she was living vicariously through my gift, but since she'd somehow managed to clue Dylan in to my power without making him think I was a total freak, I wasn't complaining. My only real complaint was that of all the people in the world for her to pick to share the family secret with, she'd picked Dylan.

I didn't answer Lexie's question. As far as I was concerned, we were right back where we had started. I knew that Mr. Kissler was doing or had done something awful, but I had no idea whatsoever where to go from there.

"We could Google him," Dylan said. Lexie looked at him closely, like she was trying to decide whether or not he'd said something dirty.

"As in the Internet?" I asked. He nodded, and I imagined him tattooing the words "Stupid Question" on my forehead.

"Good idea," Lexie said. "Why didn't we think of that?"

The three of us moved over to my computer, and I signed on, and put up my away message so I wouldn't be bothered by any Goldens who might be looking to confirm some kind of rumor they'd read about me on the bathroom wall. I typed "Jonah Kissler" into the search engine and hit Enter.

"You type with two fingers," Dylan commented.

"So?" I asked, feeling like giving him another good smack. Ever since I'd grudgingly told him that his aura seemed to shield me from the effects of Garn, he'd gotten even cockier than usual, and it was really starting to get to me.

Dylan didn't say anything because the results popped up and we were too busy reading. There was an article that had appeared in the local paper on Mr. Kissler receiving the district award for excellence in secondary school teaching, there was another article on the new hospital volunteer program, and there was a bunch of information on a woman named Jonah Kissler who lived somewhere in North Carolina and was apparently an accomplished flute player.

"Who names their little girl Jonah?" I asked. Dylan clicked on the link.

"Apparently, Mr. and Mrs. Sam Kissler of Park Meadow, North Carolina," he said. "It must be a family name."

"Jonah?" I asked incredulously. He shrugged and went back to the original search page.

"Isn't he connected to a death or a maiming or something?" I asked, getting frustrated already even though we'd barely started the search.

With a patronizing look, Dylan went up to the top of the screen and typed the word "maiming" in after Mr. Kissler's name. Nothing came up. "Imagine that," he said. "Mr. Kissler doesn't have a blog in which he confesses to maiming someone and blackening his aura for life."

"Shut up," I told him.

My away message started blinking, letting me know that someone had instant-messaged me, but I ignored it. "Try 'death,'" I told him.

He did as I instructed, and I scoffed at the way he used all his fingers to type. Lexie sat silently beside us, just watching, and I could practically see her willing herself to get her first dose of Premonition or Distance Vision.

The hospital article came up again in the search

results, and ignoring Dylan, I reached across his body and used the mouse to click on the link for the article. When the page came up, Dylan rolled his eyes.

"This is just going to tell us what a nice guy he is for volunteering at the hospital so much. I swear he's the local poster boy for medical volunteers," he muttered.

"For how long?" Lexie asked, biting her bottom lip in concentration. I wondered what she was thinking.

"Huh?" Dylan asked, sounding thoroughly male.

"How long has he been volunteering at the hospital?" my little sister asked.

"Since he came here, I guess," Dylan said. Lexie and I stared at him, waiting for him to elaborate. Finally, he did. "I guess about three years ago."

Lexie twirled her hair around one finger absentmindedly. "What was going on at the hospital back then?"

"Sickness," Dylan answered. "And, uh, surgery and blood donation and things like that."

"Blood," I whispered, thinking. "You think he's some kind of vampire or something?"

"The charming kind that goes out in the sun and volunteers at the hospital?" Lexie asked unsurely. "I don't think so."

I had to admit that it didn't sound like a very real possibility, and for someone who had accepted my Sight so easily, Dylan looked at me like I'd just suggested barbecuing his pet goat. I shook my head and told myself sternly that not everyone in Oklahoma had a pet goat.

"You don't have a pet goat, do you?" I asked him, having seemingly no control over what my mouth wanted to say.

"No," he said dryly, not elaborating any more than that.

"So if he's such a bad guy, why does he volunteer at the hospital so much?" Lexie asked. She was really stuck on that point.

"Just to make people think he's this great guy," I suggested.

"Maybe," Lexie said, but she still didn't sound like she believed it.

"Sick people can't fight back," Dylan said, his eyes darkening. "If he's some kind of predator or something, maybe he just wants to be around weak people."

Lexie shook her head. "I don't think it's that either," she said. "Not exactly." I wondered why Dylan and I were looking to my thirteen-year-old sister for answers, but I didn't bother spending much time questioning it.

"Maybe not weak people in general," I said. "Maybe a specific weak person?"

Lexie nodded her head. "But not now," she said. "Maybe someone back when he first started volunteering?"

I let out a long breath in frustration. We were just guessing, and it didn't feel like we were getting anywhere at all. "We can't very well look at everyone who's been in the hospital in the past three years," I said.

The three of us sat silently for a minute, and absentmindedly, I checked to see who had IM'd me.

"Who's beacherboya21?" Dylan asked derisively.

"Nobody," I said quickly. That was Paul's screen name. I looked at my watch. It was almost five-thirty here, which meant that school would have just let out for the day in California.

"I'll be right back," I said, fully intending to grab my mom's cell phone and take advantage of the fact that she had a national plan with no extra fees for long distance.

"Whatever," Lexie and Dylan said together. The fact that the two of them were getting along so well was starting to freak me out. Who would have thought my perky little sister and the town's resident brooder would have been on the same wavelength?

As I ran for my mom's phone, I could hear someone typing away at my keyboard, and from the speed with which the fingers flew over the keys, I knew that it had to be Dylan. Lexie typed like I did.

Fishing my mom's phone out of her purse, I dialed Paul's number. His mom answered the phone, and I had to talk to her for a full five minutes, assuring her that Oklahoma was just fine and dandy and that my mom and dad and Lexie were doing great, before she put Paul on the phone.

"I just IM'd you," he said immediately. He didn't sound terribly happy to hear from me. In fact, he sounded pretty uncomfortable. Silently, I cursed the phone. In person, I could have watched the way his lights were moving. In person, I might have stood a chance against his cryptic small talk. I could have at least

175

checked to see if we had a friend connection or a tied connection.

"Lis? I just IM'd you." He hated repeating himself.

"I know," I said. "Lexie and a friend are on my computer, so I thought I'd give you a quick call." I paused, wondering what exactly it was I'd wanted to say to him. "I've been calling. You haven't been answering." That wasn't what I'd intended to say. In fact, it was the last thing I'd wanted to say. My mouth wasn't very good about consulting my brain before speaking. In fact, I was pretty sure my mouth was out to spite me.

Paul was silent for a moment in typical Paul style. Silence was much more awkward over the phone than it was in person. Finally, he spoke. "It's weird not having you here," he said. "You've always been next door, and the people who live there now, they have younger kids."

I hadn't stopped to think that someone else had moved into my old house. That sort of put a crimp in my moving-back-to-California plan. "How's Jules?" I asked. Talking about Jules was about as far from blurting out "Are you glad you kissed me or aren't you" as I could get. Paul relaxed a little and talked more like the guy who I'd been best friends with for my entire life.

"She's good," he said. "She finally broke up with the stockbroker." I laughed. It was great to hear his voice again, and to share a private joke with somebody. Julia's latest boyfriend had been a forty-year-old in a sixteen-year-old body. He wore a tie every day, something Paul and I made fun of mercilessly. That and his affection for watching the financial channel on satellite at Jules' house had earned him the nickname of the stockbroker from Paul and me.

I groaned good-naturedly. "She had to wait until I left," I complained. Jules hadn't hung out with us much over the summer because of the stockbroker. Then again, if Jules had been around, Paul and I probably wouldn't have kissed. Looking back, I couldn't decide if that would have been a good thing or not.

"She have any new prospects yet?" I asked. Jules had a habit of having boyfriends, which was so weird to me since she wasn't a prissy girl at all and was practically fundamentally opposed to makeup.

Paul paused for a second, and I was sure he was mentally running a list of Julia's potential boy toys through his head. It took him a while to respond. "I don't think so," he said, rushing the words a little.

I didn't really pay much attention to Paul's response. It was just really good to hear his voice. It made me homesick and Paul-sick and Jules-sick all at once. If only I hadn't left, I would have been there when Jules broke up with the stockbroker, and we all could have had a good laugh about it. Then I could have asked her about Paul and me, and she would have given it to me straight. If I hadn't left . . .

Downstairs, the doorbell rang.

"Lis, will you get that?" my mom called from the

kitchen. I rolled my eyes. I was the only one in the house on the phone, and yet somehow, I was the only one capable of answering the door. Forget the fact that my sister was upstairs on my computer with a guy from my school, working on solving my mystery.

The doorbell rang again.

"Lissy," my mom yelled from downstairs.

"I have to go," I told Paul.

"Okay," he said, not sounding all that torn up about it. "We miss you around here." I wondered if that was his way of telling me that he specifically missed me.

"I miss you guys too," I told him, figuring it was a safe response. I was getting used to giving Paul safe responses.

"Bye," I said. I hung up before I had to hear Paul tell me goodbye again, and I ran down two flights of stairs to answer the door before my mom yelled for me to answer it again.

I opened the door, half expecting to see Grams or Emily or, heaven forbid, Lilah.

"Hi," Audra said cheerfully. I thought of Lexie and Dylan upstairs and wondered if taking Audra up there would be somewhat incriminating. My mom came into the room, wiping her hands on the apron she was wearing. I wondered why I had had to be the one to answer the door if she could leave whatever she was cooking in the kitchen to come in now.

I quickly made the introductions.

"You'll have to stay for dinner," my mom said, giving Audra a one-hundred-watt smile. "One of the things I missed most about leaving here when I did was not having drop-by visitors on a regular basis. In California, people are always calling first."

"That's probably because you can't walk anywhere," Audra said.

"Or because everyone has cell phones," I muttered. My mom gave me a look and then returned to the kitchen. I wondered what I was going to do with Audra between now and dinner. I didn't want to alienate the only female friend I had in this place, but I wasn't exactly in the mood for an encore of the "I Have Special Powers" show.

"Dylan instant-messaged me," Audra told me. "Are they upstairs?"

"They?" I asked, my mind racing.

"Dylan and your little sister," she told me. "Upstairs?" With that one-word question, she was walking up the stairs, and I was following her.

"Wondering what they told me?" she asked, obviously enjoying my discomfort.

"Maybe," I said.

"Everything," Lexie told me cheerfully from the top of the steps.

"The whole shebang," Dylan confirmed, coming into view.

Five minutes later, all four of us were in my room.

"Did I ever mention that I'm a hacker?" Audra asked me cheerfully. I stared at her, trying to reconcile the talkative and Tate-obsessed, slightly sarcastic girl I had met with my mental image of a computer hacker.

"No," I said. "I don't think you ever mentioned that."

Audra grinned. "Must have slipped my mind."

"Dylan thought she could hack into the hospital's database," Lexie told me, "so we told her everything."

I stared at the three of them. "And you believed them?" I asked her incredulously. "You don't just think we're all completely insane?"

Audra shrugged. "I'm not so sure about this Mr.-Kissler-being-evil thing," she said, "because he's pretty dang good-looking for a soulless guy, and I did think Dylan had lost it, but I'm always up for a hacking challenge, and your sister can be pretty persuasive."

In that moment I hoped that Lexie never got her Sight, as much as I knew she would hate it if that happened. She had a way with people that was far better than any supernatural gift, and I was starting to realize that if she got the Sight, she might lose that special something she did have. I didn't want that to happen. Maybe Lexie was better off as a Blind.

Audra sat down at my computer and her fingers flew across the keys. Dylan, Lexie, and I looked around the room, saying nothing. None of us had a clue what Audra was doing. After about three minutes, she sat back, perfectly satisfied with herself.

"Done," she said. "It just needs a few minutes to load, and then we'll have access to whatever data they've entered into their system since they updated the database a few years ago."

I stared at her. "Isn't this illegal?" I asked.

Audra didn't answer, an extremely innocent expression on her face.

"Incredibly illegal," Dylan told me.

"Look who turned into adjective boy," Audra commented to me, smirking in Dylan's general direction.

"Don't blame me," I said. I pointed at Lexie. "Blame her."

"Sure," Lexie said. "Blame the little sister."

"So, what's this about Tracy having some voodoo mojo that ties Tate to her?" Audra asked, looking extremely interested. I groaned, and Dylan did the same.

Quickly running through the explanation again, I was interrupted when the computer made a happy beeping sound.

"Is that a good sound?" I asked.

Audra tapped her fingers absentmindedly on the keys, her eyes searching the screen. "That's a very good sound," she said. "What were you guys looking for in the database?"

I looked at Dylan and my sister, and they both shrugged.

"Something incriminating?" I suggested.

Audra stared at me for a minute, and I made an executive decision. "Do they keep volunteer records?" I asked. "Like the hours that people work?"

Less than a minute later, Audra had pulled the file up on screen. I let out a low whistle. If I was reading the screen right, it looked like Mr. Kissler had volunteered three days a week for the past three years, with only a few weeks' vacation that entire time.

"Where does the evil guy go on vacation?" I asked. "And what kind of volunteer work did he do when he first started?"

"Which question do you want her to answer first?" Dylan asked reasonably. I gave him a disgruntled look. Apparently, he'd started being reasonable around the same time he'd started talking.

"The second one," I said. Audra took the mouse and clicked on some highlighted words.

"Orderly," Lexie read out loud.

"Just an ordinary volunteer," Audra clarified. "Changing sheets and bedpans, keeping patients company, that kind of thing."

I pointed to a link on the screen. "What's that?" I asked.

Audra clicked it. "Papers filed," she said. "It's a list of official documents he's turned in." Scrolling down the page, she stopped, her eyes widening.

"Certification of Death," she whispered.

"Isn't that something doctors usually sign?" Lexie asked.

Audra tried to access the document, but the computer wouldn't let her open it. She blew a wisp of hair out of her face, frustrated, and tried again without success.

"He probably just discovered that someone was dead," Dylan said.

"Maybe he killed them," I said. We both looked at Lexie. She didn't say anything at all.

Audra banged on the keys some more. Another page

popped up, but it wasn't the one she was looking for, and she ran her hands through her hair and groaned. "It won't let me in," she said. "I think you can only access it from a hospital computer. I could try reworking this one so that the system reads it as a base computer, but that could take months."

"Well, if whatever is making him all Garn-ish happened a long time ago," I said, "I guess there's not a rush."

"No," Lexie said vehemently. "We need to know now."

I gave her a little hug. She always took things to heart and threw herself into them 100 percent right away. I knew how she felt. I wasn't really feeling like giving up yet either.

I turned my attention to the screen that had popped up. "It's a patient file," I said. "This could be even better than the death Whatsit, Audra."

"Think this is the person who died?" Dylan asked.

"It's a hospital," I said reasonably. "People die all the time." My words hung in the air for a little bit, and I think everyone felt about as silly as I did. Here we were freaking out, just because Mr. Kissler had witnessed one death during his three-year stretch volunteering at the local hospital. That was hardly incriminating evidence.

Reading the file, Audra wrinkled her nose. "This woman seems perfectly healthy," she said. "A few heart problems, but she was old, so that's not incredibly unexpected." Then she paused for a long moment.

"What?" I asked, not even trying to read the information myself.

"There's another report," she said. "One on mental health." She pointed to the bottom of the paper.

I waited for her to access it, and for a solid five minutes, I could hear her punching keys like mad.

"It's no use," she said finally. "It won't let me access that one either."

"What kind of mental problems do you think she had?" I asked.

"This is ridiculous," Dylan said. "We don't even have a real lead here. Audra, you might as well check on the vacation thing Lissy was asking about earlier." I could tell from the tone in his voice that he was starting to doubt whether we'd ever be able to figure anything out about the seemingly perfect Mr. Kissler.

Halfheartedly, Audra started hacking into the closest airline's records. I was impressed, but at the rate we were going, I wasn't expecting to find out anything.

"Paul IM'd you," Lexie told me, a frown on her face. I could tell she was thinking about Kissler. I could also tell that she wasn't thinking about what she was saying out loud because she'd just mentioned something that she should have known quite well I wouldn't want mentioned.

"I called him," I said, sending her mental messages to shut up.

"California," Audra said out loud.

"Yeah," I confirmed. "Paul's a friend from California."

A friend? More than a friend? Less than a friend now that I was a million miles away?

"No," Audra said, ignoring the way Dylan was staring at me with a belligerent expression on his face, "that's where Mr. Kissler went on his last vacation. California."

I sighed. "At least he has good taste in vacation spots," I said. "He can't be all bad." Even as I said it, I knew deep down that he was, and that whatever it was that had tainted his aura wasn't a thing of the past. Closing my eyes, I could still see his aura in my mind, and it made me sick just thinking about it.

Whatever he had done, he was still doing it, and I only knew one thing for certain. Lexie had been right. Whatever was going on, we needed to figure it out. Soon.

"Dinner!" my mom yelled up the stairs. The four of us jumped, completely startled. You would have thought we were breaking the law or something.

"So I guess I'm making a trip to the hospital tomorrow," Audra said.

I stared at her like she had sprouted leaves.

"I'll go with you," Lexie offered. "We can say we want to sign up to volunteer or something. I think tomorrow's Emily's day to pick us up. I'm sure she can give us a ride, and my uncle might even be working."

I stared at Lexie. She and Audra had clearly lost their minds. A little innocent hacking from my bedroom was one thing. Trying to access documents at the hospital itself was entirely something else.

"That will give you guys something to do when we go in," Dylan said.

"Go in?" I asked.

"You heard Kissler today in class," Dylan said. "He's giving Tracy a little one-on-one attention after school tomorrow."

It was like he was trying to tell me something, but I had no idea what. Whether it was because he wasn't making sense or because my mind had gone fuzzy again, I wasn't sure.

"If he's hiding something, we should be able to find some information at his house," Dylan said.

"Dinner," my mom yelled up again.

"We can't just break into his house," I said.

"Did I ever mention Dylan has a juvenile record?" Audra asked.

I shook my head and told her that no, she'd never mentioned that.

"We aren't going to just go over there and break down his door," I hissed as the four of us walked down to dinner.

"Of course not," Dylan said. I let out a breath in relief. "People around here don't lock their doors."

I wasn't on my own anymore with the Great Math Teacher Mystery, but considering that my only two friends were both dead set on breaking the law to help me sort it out, I wasn't sure whether that was a good thing or not.

The only thing I knew for sure was that we were all in way over our heads.

13

white

Dylan and Audra didn't linger long after dinner, not that I blamed them. With the way my mom was playing a friendly round of twenty questions, I would have jetted right out of there too, especially since Lexie had absolutely no poker face whatsoever. My parents might not have been the most observant people in the world, but I was pretty sure that there was no way anyone could take a single look at my little sister and not know immediately that something was up.

"Bye," Audra said, "thanks so much for dinner. It was really nice to meet y'all." I did a double take when she said "y'all." This was the first time I'd heard her speak with any kind of accent whatsoever. My mom smiled at her words, and I wondered if Audra's intention all along had been to put my mother at ease. If so, Audra was much smoother than I could ever hope to be, and infinitely smoother than Lexie was.

Dylan mumbled something that I couldn't decipher, smiled a rare smile at each of my parents, and he and Audra made a beeline for the door. Lexie and I followed them out, the hot pink lights surrounding Lexie practically vibrating with excitement and the strain of not blurting out our plans to the entire dinner table.

"So we're going to the hospital to sign up for volunteer shifts tomorrow?" she asked Audra innocently. Audra nodded, a wicked gleam in her eye, and I wondered if I had done the right thing by getting her involved in all this. Ditto for Lexie and Dylan.

"And we're . . ." Dylan trailed off, looking around with an extremely conspicuous look on his face. Stealthy he was not.

"Never mind," I said, sure already that whatever it was that Dylan and I were going to be doing at Mr. Kissler's house while he and the Lady of the Song got their precalc on was going to be a huge mistake. I could practically feel the word "grounded" being engraved on my forehead, and not in nice, scripty calligraphy letters either.

"We'll see you tomorrow," Lexie promised them both. After my friends left, I turned to look at her.

"Why did I let you talk me into this?" I asked her.

"You act like you had a choice about all this," she said as she grinned at me. "We needed their help. I can tell just by looking at you that the Garn sitch is bad, and you'll die if you don't do something."

I thought that was a little melodramatic, but given

my penchant for losing my lunch around Mr. Kissler, perhaps it wasn't that much of an overstatement. "And we needed them why?" I asked her.

Lexie shrugged, her pink aura moving gracefully up and then back down again with the motion. "Beats me why," she told me, "but we do need them." She paused for a moment, a thoughtful and well-practiced look on her face. "And whatever Audra did on your computer was wicked cool," she added.

It was on the tip of my tongue to ask if she'd known Audra was going to be able to do that. Maybe little sis had gotten a sudden dose of Premonition or something. Still, I couldn't bring myself to ask, because I'd probably just get Lexie's hopes up. She was obsessed enough that I was sure the entire world, or at the very least our immediate family, would know the second she showed signs of any Sight.

"Wicked cool," I agreed, feeling like a complete idiot, more for the fact that I was using teen lingo with an outrageous imitation of an Oklahoma accent than because I'd used the word "wicked" in the first place.

"You really think we'll get away with all this?" I asked Lexie.

She looked at me, not cracking a grin. "Not a chance," she told me seriously, "but we've got to try."

I didn't particularly like the sound of that, and unconsciously, I rubbed my forehead, which, to my relief, hadn't been engraved quite yet.

"I'm going upstairs," I told Lexie, wanting to escape before she thought to ask me about Paul. I really wasn't in the mood for a Paul discussion, especially since I'd yet to talk with him about the kiss, and my sixth sense (or maybe it was my seventh sense, given the whole advance Sight thing) was firmly telling me that he wasn't exactly waiting around the old neighborhood for me to come back.

I rubbed my temples slightly as I climbed the stairs, walked into my room, and flopped down on my bed with an inhuman groan. Life here was so much more complicated than life in California had been, my mom's involvement with high-profile police cases aside.

In California, I hadn't had to worry about mysteries like this one, or, for that matter, about senile and out-spoken old women who spoke in single-word commands, dressed in orange muumuus, and invited random guys to eat dinner at my house. Rolling over onto my side, I hugged my pillow to my chest and closed my eyes. It had been a long day, and all I really wanted was a moment of silence.

I was surrounded by darkness. Looking around, I could see nothing, but I could feel the wrongness of it all in the air. Why couldn't I see? I was blind and terrified, and the earth was shaking beneath me.

I blinked several times. The darkness was familiar. I'd been here before. I'd seen this before, the same darkness, the same wrongness in the air. I searched my memory and came up empty-handed, but with a soothing sense of déjà vu, I looked over my shoulder, waiting. I had no idea what I was waiting for.

Then an unearthly light filled the space, and I saw a figure walking toward me. Ah, yes, the mysterious woman in white, surrounded by a pearly white light. I paused for a moment. Her aura was the same color as Dylan's. That was certainly strange.

As she walked closer, the light became too bright for my eyes, accustomed to darkness, and I closed them.

With cool hands she touched my eyelids.

Even with my eyes closed, images flew through my mind at great speed, as if I was watching them in the air in front of me: Mom and Grams with their eyes closed and their faces covered in darkness, shadows and light, shadows and light, an empty bed and lips that couldn't speak, just beginning to crack. Shadows and light. Shadows and light. Colors of every variety, every shade imaginable, everyone connected by the light, the connections pushing back the shadows. Lexie. Three intertwining circles, rings of different colors on a silver shield. Paul and Jules. What were they doing?

The images flew through my head too quickly for me to think about them coherently, and in the next moment, Paul and Jules were gone, and the cool hands were gently lifted off my eyelids.

I looked into eyes very much the same color as my own, framed by longer and darker eyelashes. Dark hair surrounded her face, and the pearl light shined brilliantly. Behind her, some kind of silver tapestry hung, with stitching so tiny that all I could make out was the three intertwining circles.

"Who are you?" I asked, cursing myself mentally for wasting her time with such a stupid question. "What do I need to know? Are you trying to tell me something?"

The woman stared at me, saying nothing, a kind expression on her face, her mouth softening into a light smile as she looked at me.

"They cannot see," I heard a voice say, even though her lips had not moved. "You must remove the shadow so that they can see the light. They will see if you remove the blindfold. She has always seen. You can see. You see what you want to see. The Champion. You will see."

As far as I could tell, there was a whole lot of see-talking going on, but I was still confused. In the next moment, she disappeared, and a single word hung in the air.

Shannon.

See. Remember. Know.

"Lissy, the bus leaves in twenty minutes," my mom yelled from downstairs. I rolled over onto my back and opened my eyes. What was she talking about? The bus for where? I looked at my watch.

It was seven-twenty-five. Hadn't we finished dinner at six-thirty? I stretched, my body incredibly stiff. I felt as if I had been asleep for hours.

Someone knocked on my door, and I rolled off the bed and answered it.

"Lissy," my little sister hissed before I could even say anything. "We're leaving for school in nineteen minutes. Today's the day you have to go with Dylan, and I'm going to the hospital with Audra. I thought maybe we could talk about things for a few minutes first, and we'd better do it quick, because Grams is downstairs, and she wants to talk to you. Why are you still wearing your clothes from yesterday?"

My eyes widened, and my brain slowly shifted into gear. "What do you mean yesterday?" I asked. "I was only asleep for an hour."

"Thirteen hours," Lexie corrected me. "It's Thursday morning. D-day, as in detective, as in mystery, as in goodbye, law-abiding citizens, hello, hacking and breaking and entering."

She was babbling and her aura was doing pretty much the same thing, waving in frantic little rolls as she spoke.

"I had a dream," I said, walking over to my closet, still in a daze, to look for something to wear that wasn't wrinkled and embarrassingly spotted with drool.

"What kind of dream?" Lexie asked, leaning against the wall, a grin on her face. For once in her life, she was ready before I was. I grabbed a shirt and, after ditching my sticky-with-sweat shirt from the day before, pulled the clean one over my head.

"Shannon," I said simply, "and something about blindfolds. Shadows and light, and this weird symbol I keep seeing with a few rings or something like that."

Even I had to admit that I sounded somewhat cryptic, but then again, the dream hadn't exactly been straightforward.

"Shannon?" Lexie practically shrieked. "You have got to be kidding me. Some people have all the luck. Don't tell me you just got a visitation. I've never gotten one, and neither has Mom, and I don't even think Grams has."

I wanted to smack myself in the forehead for mentioning it to her at all. "It was just a dream," I said firmly, "albeit a really strange one. I've had the strangest dreams since we moved here."

I barely had time to pull on a pair of clean jeans and switch shoes before my grandmother's voice boomed through the house.

"Lesson!"

My eyes rolled back in my head. "This is not happening," I muttered. "The last time she gave me a 'lesson' was when all this started, more or less. It's not like she even listened when I tried to tell her about the Garn guy, and now she wants to give me another lesson?"

Lexie shrugged. "Some people have all the luck," she repeated, sighing.

"Now!" Grams was getting impatient.

Grabbing my book bag, I headed down the stairs, and with each step I took, I reflashed as my memory threw image after image at me. Step, shadows, step, light. Step. Garn. Step.

"It's about time," Grams huffed the second I came into the kitchen. "We've got work to do, Felicity Shannon James."

Shannon. The name echoed in my mind, and this time, I had an image to go with it. She'd had dark hair, much darker than any of ours, and a voice that spoke without her moving her lips.

"Grams," I said slowly as I sat down at the table beside her. "Have you ever had a . . ." What had Lexie called it? "Have you ever had a visitation?"

Grams narrowed her eyes at me and leaned across the table. "A visitation? From a power?"

I looked down at my hands. They trembled a little as I spoke, and my almost-silver aura rolled with the motion. "Not exactly," I said. "I mean, have you ever had a visitation thing from Shannon?"

"The First Seer?" Grams asked. Now why couldn't I have a cool title like that?

I nodded. "Like in a dream or something," I told her. "Has she ever come to you in a dream? Ever said anything to you?"

"Lissy girl," Grams said. "In the more than three hundred years since she died, fifteen generations and more, only a handful have ever heard her voice again or seen through her infinitely blessed eyes."

"Infinitely blessed?"

"All our gifts: clairvoyance, aura vision, premonition, retronition, pure vision, true vision, heart vision . . ." Grams trailed off. "All come from her. She had them all."

I let out a low whistle, just imagining what it must have been like for her to see with those eyes. "But some people have seen her?" I asked. "Since she died, she has visited or whatever, right?"

Grams nodded. "Her daughters," she said softly. "Her three daughters, and occasionally after that, their children and their children's children and *their* children and on down the line in times of great need."

I looked down at the table, my voice caught in my throat. If this wasn't a time of great need, I didn't know what was.

"What are you trying to say, child?" Grams said. "Have you—? Did she—?"

I cleared my throat. "Remember when I was telling you about what happened at school?" I asked. I didn't wait for her to respond before I plowed on. "About what I saw that day I got sick?"

Grams waved her hand dismissively, and a shadow flashed across her aura. "Not that nonsense again," she said.

My heart sank. "You need to listen to me," I told her. "It isn't nonsense, and something horrible is going on at the school. Mr. Kissler—"

She cut me off. "Jonah Kissler is a wonderful man."

"You don't understand," I said. "What I see when I look at him, it's worse than death, Grams, it's like . . . like he doesn't have a soul, and just looking at him, it hurts and—"

"Jonah Kissler is a wonderful man," she said again. Her dampened aura stood perfectly still.

I shut my mouth. There was no way I could tell her about my dream, about Shannon, not when all she could say was that Jonah Kissler, whose every movement made my stomach roll, was a wonderful, wonderful man.

"Sure, Grams," I said. "Whatever."

"Now that we've settled that silly business, why the sudden curiosity about the First Seer? You've never shown an interest before, not like Lexie." Grams looked at me.

"I was just wondering," I said.

"Why?" she shot back. My grandmother was perceptive, but why was it that the one thing I really needed her to grasp, she couldn't?

"No reason," I said.

The silence that followed was broken when my mom breezed through the room. "Ride's leaving," she said. "We still have to pick up Lilah." I gritted my teeth at the mention of Lilah's name. With everything that I was dealing with, my mom didn't want to make poor Lilah late. How thoughtful of her.

"You owe me a lesson, child," Grams said as I stood up from the table.

"And you owe me one, Grams," Lexie said reproachfully, coming into the room. I shot her a grateful look. I so wasn't in the mood for a Grams lecture right now. If there was one thing that talking to her had convinced me of, it was that I was on my own and wouldn't get any help from her.

With my backpack slung over my shoulder, I walked quickly out the front door, Lexie at my heels.

"Don't forget to tell Mom you're going home with Dylan," Lexie hissed as the two of us piled into the car.

"Oh yeah," I said out loud. "Mom, I'm going over to Dylan's after school today to hang out." Even to my ears, that sounded extremely lame, and I totally didn't think she was going to buy it.

"That's nice, honey," my mom said, a smile in her voice. I wondered what she thought she was smiling about, and figured that she probably thought I had my sights set on Dylan. No pun intended. The idea was laughable in itself, though, because Dylan was not my kind of guy in the least. Thinking of guys made me think of Paul, thinking of Paul made me think of Jules, and thinking of Paul and Jules made me think of my mega-weird dream.

I was so busy thinking that I barely noticed when Lilah climbed into the car.

"Did your mom get my message?" Lexie asked her immediately.

Lilah nodded. "She's going to drop you and me and Lissy's little friend off at the hospital this afternoon."

Even though there was some kind of mild distaste in her voice, Lilah's aura didn't do the hissing dance when she talked about Audra. That was a start. It took me a second to register what she had said.

"You're going with them to the hospital?" I squeaked.

Lilah looked at me sideways, arching her perfectly plucked eyebrows slightly. "Yes," she said, clearly mystified as to why I cared. "I haven't given blood in a while, and to-day is as good a time as any."

I exchanged a look with Lexie. This was definitely a hitch in our plan. The last thing Audra needed when she was trying to break into the hospital files was Lilah hovering around. Lilah hated Audra. Hadn't she warned me against her the first day?

I took this all as a very clear sign that things just were not going to go my way today. Lexie shrugged it off. I could practically see her saying "Oh well" in a perfectly cheerful voice.

I took a deep breath. Whether or not Lilah's presence was going to complicate the hospital side of our little illegal maneuver wasn't really my major concern. After all, Dylan and I were going to have our hands absolutely full.

As usual, the car fell silent when my mom dropped Lexie off at the middle school.

"So how's school, Lilah?" my mom asked, filling the silence with her cheerful question.

"It's all right," Lilah said, and even though her voice sounded perfectly convincing, as if she was having the time of her life, the purple lights surrounding her body didn't move at all. Whatever she was feeling, Lilah wasn't excited about the prospect of another day at school. I wondered if Lilah was one of those people who was never happy. What did she have to be so unexcited about? She was popular, had a steady boyfriend who was cute and a midnight blue, and her hair had never even thought of tangling. Compounded by the fact that I was pretty sure Lilah didn't have problems with cryptic dreams—I wondered why exactly she wasn't laughing diabolically at the prospect of another day in high school.

I didn't waste much time getting out of the car once we pulled up to school. "I can walk home from Dylan's," I told my mom, even though I had no idea whatsoever whether that was true or not. I'd been told a million times already that this was a small town. Surely I could walk home.

"Hey, Lissy," Lilah said as we walked away from the car. It surprised me that she would even talk to me. "Tracy's really weird when it comes to Tate. I wouldn't mess with him if I were you, because you don't want to mess with her, and for some reason, she thinks you're like majorly into him or something. Plus with the whole Colin and what's-her-name thing, she's going all schizo on any Non who even looks at Tate."

I stared at Lilah. She was acting as if (a) I was somehow unaware of Tracy's hostility, and (b) she, Lilah, didn't totally pull the mother bear routine whenever another girl even looked at Brock.

I guess my dream had been right about one thing. People only saw what they wanted to see, and Lilah clearly didn't see herself the way I saw her.

"I don't want Tate," I said. "And you can tell Tracy that."

Lilah shrugged and put on a pair of sunglasses. "It's

not like you guys could date anyway," she mumbled, walking off with a cool strut. I so totally did not understand that girl.

Today I didn't have any problems walking through the tangle of connections in the front lawn. I didn't so much as stumble when I threw my bag down next to Audra and Dylan and sat.

"You ready for this?" Dylan asked me. For the moment, I ignored him, mostly because there was no planet on which the answer to that question was yes.

"You and Lexie are going to have a little company," I told Audra.

She narrowed her eyes at me suspiciously.

"Lilah," I said, not even waiting for her question. Audra groaned. She was understandably thrilled.

"Lexie can handle her," I promised Audra, hoping it was true. "You just need a little alone time with a hospital computer, right?"

Audra sighed. "I'd been hoping to have Lexie as a lookout," she said. "Not as a Lilah distracter. And allow me to reemphasize the evil incarnate thing. Definitely not optimal research conditions."

I shrugged. I knew better than anyone, we didn't always get what we wanted.

"You ready?" Dylan asked me again, turning to face me a little more. In the morning sun, the pearly white from his face was strikingly bright, and I flashed back to my dream for a minute. Hadn't Shannon, the infamous

First Seer, been the same color as Dylan? I wondered if that meant we were somehow related, and even though I wasn't sure why, I spent a few seconds devoutly hoping that wasn't true.

The sound of singing saved me from answering. I stared across the lawn, watching as Tracy sang to Tate. So much for subtlety. She wasn't even waiting for music class anymore.

Immediately, I felt myself leaving my body, and my ghost self was on the Golden side of the lawn in a flash, standing directly between Tracy and Tate. I threw up my hands and opened my mouth to scream, but no sound came out, as a thick, purple cord of light flew right through my stomach.

Surprisingly enough, I couldn't feel it at all, and, only mildly disconcerted, I turned around to watch Tracy's aura lasso in action.

The cord attacked Tate, wrapping itself around his waist and pulling him toward her. For an insane instant, I got the feeling that Tracy was going to eat him, but I dismissed the notion as a by-product of too many late nights watching B-movies with Paul and Jules.

"Is she doing it again?" I heard a voice ask in a whisper from far away. I didn't respond, caught in the middle of whatever was going on between Tracy and Tate.

A few seconds later, Tracy stopped singing, and I was able to step out of the entanglement that was her new connection to Tate. This time, several of Tracy's aura strings were tied around several of Tate's, and his struggled madly against hers. I lifted up my hand, thinking to free him from her grasp—it wasn't like she was playing fair anyway—but something stopped me.

Turning in my ghost body, I looked across the lawn. Standing there, near where my *body* body was, was Mr. Kissler, as Garn-covered as ever. He was staring directly at me, and not the real me either. His eyes locked on my ghost eyes, and for a second, I couldn't move at all.

"Lissy?" Audra's voice said. "Is she doing it again? What do you see?"

Her voice snapped me out of it, and I jumped back into my body, my eyes fluttering open. Cautiously, I looked around for Mr. Kissler. I felt his eyes on me, and when I met them, this time in my real body, I felt my face blushing, and my ears started to roar. Without being told to, Dylan took my hands and shifted his weight so that he partially blocked my view of the math teacher.

I stared at the pearl white on his face, and for a moment, I thought I saw a small prism of color underneath. Slowly, my nausea and dizziness subsided. In a shaky voice, I answered Audra's question. "Yeah," I said softly, still holding Dylan's hands, "she did it again."

Audra ground her foot into the floor a little. "He was probably getting ready to break up with her too," she said glumly.

"What a travesty," Dylan muttered.

Audra narrowed her eyes at him and then turned the

look at me. "I blame you." I stared at her, shocked. What exactly was she blaming me for anyway? It wasn't as if I was the one who had told Tracy to go all singing seductress on Tate. "He never used to talk this much," Audra said.

"I blame Lexie," I said, not feeling the least bit guilty for using my younger sister as a scapegoat. *And Grams,* my inner voice added silently. I knew it was bad when my conscience started picking on my grandmother instead of telling me not to.

Even with Dylan sitting in front of me, I could feel Kissler's eyes on me, and I shuddered. Did he know something was up? I could have sworn that he had seen my ghostly self standing there, but that was impossible. No one could see me when I went all ghostlike.

If he had seen me, there was a distinct possibility that all of us were in more trouble than we wanted to admit.

"You ready for today?" Dylan asked me yet again.

I let myself fall back on the grass with a frustrated sigh. Looking up at the sky, I took a deep breath.

"I guess I'm about as ready as I'm going to be," I said.

Dylan smirked. "Good enough," he said as the warning bell rang. Audra reached down to pull me up off the ground, and the three of us walked into the school building together. I had a feeling I was in over my head, but at least now, for better or worse, I wasn't alone.

14

silver

The moment the bell rang at the end of math, I was out the door.

"You know, you can be really fast when you want to be," Dylan muttered, catching up to me.

"If you saw what I saw," I told him, "you'd be fast too."

Dylan smirked at me through the hair in his face, and I knew without a doubt that he was replaying the scene I'd told him about his aura shielding me from the Garn.

The Champion.

"What's with the look?" Dylan asked as I grimaced.

"Nothing," I said. "Just thinking about a dream I had, that's all."

"That's never all," he said, and then he did the hair-smirking thing again.

"Lissy, I'm sort of in a hurry here, so if you see your little friend, tell her that my mom, Lexie, and I are waiting, okay? Thanks." Lilah's voice broke the tension between Dylan and me. I couldn't help but notice that her "thanks" was less of an expression of gratitude than it was popularese for "Die, freak, die."

I turned to answer her, but in a flash of purple-y goodness, she was gone.

"She's a charmer, that one," Dylan said under his breath.

I snorted. "Look who's talking." I dropped my voice to a whisper. "Now are we going to do this thing or not?"

From under the too-long hair, he glanced up and down the hallway, and then he looked back at me and nodded. "Let's do it," he said. As we walked out of the school, he fell into silence, and the longer we walked, the more I felt like this plan, if you could even call it a plan, was doomed to failure.

Fifteen minutes of silent walking later, we were standing on the front lawn of a cute white house. Kissler's house.

"Don't just stand there," Dylan said, finally breaking his silence. "The longer we're outside, the bigger the chance that someone will see us."

I took a step toward the house and then paused.

"What?" he asked.

"What are we expecting to really find?" I asked him. "I mean, you don't get it, Dylan. You don't know what he is. Either we're not going to find anything and we're just going to get ourselves in a lot of trouble that I really don't need, or we're about to walk into the lair of a monster." I paused. "He *is* a monster," I said. "Don't forget that."

Dylan said nothing, but he nodded, and together, the two of us walked onto the porch and to the front door. I held my breath as Dylan reached his hand toward the doorknob. The door creaked as he opened it, and a second later, the two of us were standing inside, the door shut firmly behind us. The sound of the door closing made me jump a little, even though I had seen Dylan close it.

I looked around at the taupe walls and the crisply painted white moldings near the ceiling. Cautiously, I took a step forward and walked into the living room, pausing only to look into the kitchen on my right. The entire place was as neat as a pin, and the living room had a disturbingly homey feel to it.

"Somehow," I said out loud, wrinkling my nose a little, "this isn't quite what I expected."

Dylan wandered into the kitchen. "You didn't expect flowered dish towels?" he asked, smirking with half of his mouth in an expression that was strangely flattering.

"I was picturing something a little more dark and gloomy," I muttered. Even though it was ridiculous, I'd expected to come in here and immediately see something extremely incriminating. I wasn't really sure what that incriminating piece of information would be, but I was pretty sure I'd know it when I found it.

"Something evil?" Dylan asked in a yell from the kitchen. Even though he had no expression in his voice, I could tell he was making fun of me. I stuck my tongue out in the general direction of the kitchen, sure that any second the police were going to break down the door and catch me in my math teacher's house with my tongue hanging out of my mouth.

I wandered aimlessly through the living room, picking up magazines, flipping through them, and placing them carefully back where I'd found them. I was a little disappointed that none of the magazines had any cryptic messages written in the margins. If my life had been a TV show, there would have been notes in the margins, or a trace of blood on the carpet, or *something*. As it was, my end of the search was turning up a whole lot of nothing, and I was pretty sure that Dylan was faring more or less the same.

In the corner of the room, there was a computer, and hesitantly, I walked over and turned it on. Like Mr. Evil was going to keep computer records of all his heinous deeds. I snorted at the thought of it, but I sat down at the computer, ready to put my two-finger typing skills to work.

The computer beeped at me, and I jumped about a foot in the air, expecting to feel someone's hands wrap around my throat. I was pretty sure that my overactive imagination was my grandmother's fault, because lately everything was. If she'd believed me, we wouldn't be going through all this right now.

As soon as the computer booted up, it asked me for a password, and that was the end of the line with me and Mr. Kissler's computer.

Dylan strolled into the room. "I found a box of

newspaper clippings," he said, holding up his bounty, "but they're all about what a nice fellow he is. The guy must be the biggest narcissist I've ever met."

Dylan left the room again, and tentatively, I returned my attention to the computer, wishing that Audra was here to do her hacking brilliance thing. I tapped my finger on my chin.

If I was an evil math teacher, what would my password be? I asked myself silently. My inner voice provided no answer.

A lot of help you are, I told it silently, but it still didn't respond.

Deciding it was worth a try, I typed in evil_einstein, but just my luck, that wasn't the password. I hadn't really thought it was going to be, but still, I was hoping that maybe my visitation, if it had really been a visitation from Shannon, had left me a little more charmed than usual.

I heard Dylan scoffing audibly from a few rooms over, and, giving up on my future as a computer hacker, I stood up and followed the sounds of his derisive snorts. "Find anything?" I called as I walked down the hallway, trying to forget that I was in someone else's house illegally.

"Apparently he sews," Dylan said.

Turning the corner, I saw Dylan standing in the middle of a small room at the end of the hallway. When I entered the room, I saw exactly what Dylan had been snorting about. Our Mr. Kissler had himself a nice little sewing room, complete with several piles of fabric and a sewing machine. I had a hard time reconciling that with the image I had of him as some kind of bringer of mass destruction and undiluted evil.

With the way things were going, Mr. Perfect was probably sewing something for the hospital or making clothes for Mongolian orphans. Whatever his current sewing project was, I was willing to bet that it had saintlike written all over it.

"Think he sewed that?" Dylan asked, gesturing to a wall with one hand while he dug through the sewing drawers with another. I followed the direction of his gesture and gasped at what I saw.

"Pretty, huh?" Dylan asked cynically.

The entire wall was covered with what looked to be a hand-sewn silver tapestry, with stitches so small they were practically invisible despite the fact that the thread was colored. There, on the tapestry, were three intertwining circles, rings of different colors on a silver background.

"I've seen this before," I told Dylan. He didn't pay much attention as he pulled out a pair of sewing scissors and snipped them a couple of times.

"Dylan!" I said, ready to smack him for not paying attention to me. He turned at the tone of my voice, and I gestured toward the tapestry, my hand shaking a little as I did.

"He get it out of some catalog or something?" he asked, still holding the scissors.

I shook my head and closed my eyes for a moment.

"Ever since I came here," I said finally, "I've been having these really weird dreams, and in all of them, there was this shield, a silver shield, and on the shield there were these rings, and they looked just like these." I took a deep breath. "And last night, there was a woman, I think she might have been one of my ancestors or something." Dylan looked bored, and I wished that Lexie was there to tell him for me. I continued with my story, taking a step toward the tapestry as I did. "She was trying to tell me something, but I couldn't understand her. She was standing in front of a tapestry that looked just like this one, rings and all."

I paused for a moment, remembering some of the words she had spoken to me without ever moving her lips.

You will see, my inner voice reminded me. That was what Shannon had said.

I ran my fingertips along the edge of the tapestry, and gathering the fabric in my hands, I pulled on it with all my strength.

"What are you doing?" Dylan asked, alarm entering his voice. The fact that his voice had any inflection at all should have told me that my action was really freaking him out, but that was the last thing on my mind.

"Help me tear this down," I said. He stared at me like I'd confessed to being a closet necrophiliac. I stamped my foot. "Just do it, Dylan," I told him, my tone making it perfectly clear that I wasn't above smacking him again if he proved difficult.

"So much for being stealthy," he muttered, but he

came over and helped me, and together, we managed to tear the tapestry from the wall, revealing a sliding door.

Dylan looked at me with an expression in his eyes that might have been admiration. "How did you know?" he asked. "I thought your power was just the aura thingy."

I just loved it when people referred to my power as a thingy.

"Visitation," I mumbled, answering Dylan's question as I reached forward to slide the door sideways. To my relief it opened, and Dylan and I walked into the hidden room. "I saw it in my dreams."

The room was filled with boxes, the walls lined with papers handwritten in Mr. Kissler's neat all-caps script.

Dylan dug through the papers and let out a low whistle. "This guy is nuts," he said, handing me a couple of sheets. I looked at them, absentmindedly. Written on them were dozens of names, with notes written to the side: numbers and scrawled words I didn't understand.

"What's pyrokinesis?" I asked. Dylan shrugged, and a moment later, I heard his voice catch in his throat.

"Lissy," he said. "Isn't this a picture of your mom?"

Startled, I dropped the list of names I was skimming and knelt down next to Dylan. The picture had been taken back on the beach in California, sometime last summer by the look of my mom's haircut.

"What's wrong with her face?" I asked, wrinkling my forehead. In the picture, my mom's face was covered with black. "Marker?" I speculated. Dylan ran his thumb over the surface of the picture and shook his head.

"Some kind of tar," he said. Taking the picture from his hands, I rubbed at it, the black gooey stuff coming off on my hands. I sniffed my fingers and *really* wished I hadn't. The tar smelled like dead things.

Laying the picture on the ground, I scratched away at the tar with my fingernails, and finally, my mom's face was visible. I stared at the picture for a moment, wondering why this man would have had a picture of my mother and why he had defaced it. Dylan was right. Mr. Kissler was crazy, but looking around the room, I wondered if there wasn't more to it.

I picked the list back up and read more of the notes. "Pyrokinesis, telekinesis, telepathy, spell magic, distance vision, morphism . . ." My voice trailed off. I was holding a list of powers, supernatural powers like the Sight. Suddenly, I knew why my mom's face had been covered by tar in that picture. It wasn't so much a matter of covering her face as it had been a matter of covering her eyes.

Shannon had told me that they couldn't see because of the blindfold. Suddenly, everything was making sense.

"Shadows and light," I said out loud.

"What?" Dylan turned to look at me.

"Shadows and light," I said. "Ever since we got here, my mom's lights have looked really funny. When I look at her, I feel like I'm wearing sunglasses because her aura's just more shadowy than normal, and when I was trying to tell Grams about Mr. Kissler . . ." Grams' aura had been distinctly shadowed too. No wonder she hadn't believed me. He'd done something to her, to both of them. They were in the shadows, and no matter how hard I tried to make them understand, they couldn't see the light.

I turned to Dylan. "There should be a picture of my grandmother," I told him. "Find it." My hands were shaking as I stared back down at the master list I held. Several of the names had been crossed out.

Dottie Fleming: telekinetic
Linda Jones: hereditary mage
Cody Park: pyrokinetic

"Cody Park," I whispered, and my mind whirled. "Cody Park." We'd moved halfway across the country to get away from the murder my mom hadn't been able to stop, and now I was standing in the murderer's house.

I looked at Dylan, and my throat clamped almost closed.

"What?" he asked.

I thought of my mom, reflashing and suffering. "Cody Park."

15

prism

For the longest time, I stood there, looking at the list in my hands, gripping it so hard that my knuckles turned white. Dylan looked at me.

"He was just a little kid," I said. "Just an ordinary little kid." Only, if the notes I held were to be believed, he wasn't an ordinary little kid at all. He'd had a power, whatever pyrokinesis was. Now he was dead. My mom had seen his body, had known where to find it, but she hadn't seen his death, or his kidnapping. She hadn't seen in time to help, and now I knew why.

Her eyes had been covered, but it wasn't until we stepped foot in the town where the murderer lived that the magical blindfold had shown itself in her aura. Why hadn't I seen it before? Why hadn't I realized the second I saw it that something was wrong?

"Find the picture of Grams, Dylan," I said again,

looking back at the list. Why was Mr. Kissler killing people with powers? Was he planning on killing my mom or Grams? What about me?

I looked around. I was obviously holding one of Mr. Kissler's already-done lists, but that wasn't what I was interested in. I wanted to know what he was doing now. There was still something, something I couldn't quite put my finger on.

Violently, I flung open a filing cabinet in the corner, and I ignored the files with my mom's name on them, with Cody's name on them. When I saw the file in the back, I inhaled quickly and clarity rushed over me.

"Found it," Dylan said. I didn't react.

How was it that I'd forgotten all about the way the Garn streams had seemed to chase Tracy? How was it that I hadn't remembered, even when I'd seen her with him later, even when I'd known I was forgetting something, that it was the fact that his aura had been after hers?

You only see what you want to see.

How many times had I been told that? I hadn't seen that Tracy was involved, hadn't remembered, because I hadn't wanted to. I didn't want to see her as a victim, not when she made me one without giving it a second thought.

You only see what you want to see.

Dylan walked over behind me and watched as I opened the file marked with Tracy's name.

"What's a Siren?" he asked.

"'A mythological being whose voice has a hypnotic

216

power,'" I read, flipping through the pages in the folder. "'Sirens were thought to lure men to their deaths using their unearthly, beautiful singing voices, or to enslave men with their songs.'"

Dylan stared at me, still not getting it.

"Think about it, Dylan," I said, rolling my eyes. "What if a modern-day Siren wasn't all about luring a guy to his death? Hello!" I reached over and knocked on his head with my fist. "Enslaving a person with singing? As in singing and tying a guy to you. Doesn't this ring any bells?"

"Tracy," he said, finally getting it. I nodded and flipped the file closed, allowing him to see Tracy's name marked clearly on the cover.

You only see what you want to see.

"Lissy?" The sound of someone calling my name broke into my thoughts, and I jumped about a foot in the air. "Back here," I yelled, stepping back out into the open and leaving the hidden room full of death behind me.

I still couldn't understand why. Why would he kill people with powers? Did he hate us that much?

Hadn't I hated my own power? I banished the thought.

Walking into the hallway, Dylan on my heels, I ran smack into Audra.

"What did you find?" I asked her.

"Kissler was there at the time of death, all right," she said. "The patient's name was Linda Jones, and she was in

217

the mental health wing, of all places. She was elderly and delusional."

Remembering her name from the list, I looked directly at Audra. "Let me guess," I said. "She thought she had some sort of magical power?"

Audra nodded. "Listen, I have to tell you something else," she said quickly.

"She wasn't crazy," I said softly. "She did have a power. That's why he killed her."

"No offense, but, hello! Powers? Crazyville: population you guys," a voice said, and Lilah walked into the hallway.

I glared at Audra.

"I told you I had something to tell you," she said sheepishly.

"Lilah's on our side," Lexie said, coming into the room.

"Whatever," Lilah and I muttered at the exact same time. She glared at me for a second and then spoke again. "I could never be one of them." Her voice was soft as she folded her arms over her chest, her aura vibrating slightly.

The sight of her purple aura jolted me back into the reality we needed to face. "Tracy," I said out loud.

Lilah gave me a disgruntled look. "What about her?" she asked. "She's still at school." The "and she still thinks you're trying to get in her boyfriend's pants" part of Lilah's sentence went unsaid.

For a moment, silence settled over the room.

"With Kissler," Dylan and I said at once.

"We have to get over there, now," I said, rushing past Lilah and Lexie and out the front door.

"Is somebody going to tell me what's going on?" Lilah asked. "Like why you guys are here to begin with, or why Lexie made me come?"

I made a mental note to kill my little sister for dragging Lilah into this.

"Kissler," I said, by way of explanation. "He killed that old woman. He killed Cody Park."

"Who?" Audra asked.

Lexie stared at me, her eyes widening. I could tell by the look on her face that things were starting to fall into place in her mind. She knew exactly who Cody Park was.

"But Cody was just a little boy," Lexie said, her voice small. "He killed a little boy." The second the words were out of her mouth, Lexie paled. "It's true," she said. "He killed that little boy, and then we had to move, and . . ." She paused.

"It's his fault we're here," I said, my mind clearing just from having listened to Lexie say it all out loud. "And now we've got to stop him. He's killing people with powers." Lilah rolled her eyes. I ignored her. "Tracy's next on his list. She's a Siren." I turned to look at them. "And he's at the school with her right now. Will one of you please show me the way to get there?" They stood there looking at me.

"Now!" I roared. If I'd seen earlier, if I'd *wanted* to see earlier . . . I didn't let myself go there.

"We have to get to the school now," I hissed. "If we don't get there, he'll kill her."

"He'll kill her," Lexie echoed, going even paler, and as the words left her mouth, the truth seemed to sink into everyone's minds and thrust them into action as we headed for the school, for Tracy, and for Kissler.

I didn't so much as pause to think about what I was going to do once I got there.

Dylan led the way, and the four of us girls followed him. My feet hit the pavement hard as I broke into a run, and all I could think about was the fact that I should have seen this coming, and the only person I had to blame for the fact that I hadn't was me.

Beside me, Lilah complained with every step she took. "You people really are freaks," she said, running out of breath as we turned a corner. "A Siren? What's a Siren? Tracy's not anything but a Golden girl with a Golden guy. That's just the way things go. Accept. Deal. Move on in your little lives or whatever it is you people do."

Audra snorted a little, but wisely, she didn't say anything. I wasn't quite so wise.

"Tate doesn't want to be with Tracy," I said, and I realized that, despite everything, I was still glad to say it. I pushed the feeling down. "She's got him all nice and trapped with that pretty singing voice of hers. She sings, and it pulls him in, and he can't get away, whether he wants to or not."

"But that's not what's important," Lexie said. "At

220

least, that's not important now. What *is* important is that Tracy's in trouble, and if we don't stop it, no one will." The clock was ticking.

My lungs tightened, protesting as I pushed myself through the final leg of the run and stormed into the school building. Without waiting for the others, I charged toward Mr. Kissler's room, my hair flying behind me as I ran. Putting my hand on the doorknob, I heard voices inside: one male, and one female. I couldn't tell what either of them was saying, but it sure didn't sound like anything along the lines of "Please don't kill me" or "Prepare to die."

The others caught up to me, and their presence pushed me into turning the doorknob and throwing open the door. So much for subtlety. Stealthy I was not.

"I couldn't possibly," Tracy was saying, looking at the math teacher through batting eyelashes.

"I've heard so much about your voice," Mr. Kissler said in response. "It's all Miss Cutler can talk about in the teachers' lounge. Sing for me."

As the door slammed into the wall, Kissler turned to look at us, and seeing his dead aura head-on, knowing what it meant, I stumbled backward. Strong arms caught me and held me up, and I turned my face to look into Dylan's. The pearly white light settled me, and Dylan, knowing I was steady on my feet, walked around to stand in front of me, turning so that whenever Kissler was in my line of vision, Dylan was too.

I shot him a grateful look, and though his facial

expression didn't actually change at all, I got the feeling that he was giving me his "What now?" scowl.

"What are you freaks doing here?" Tracy asked, clearly perturbed that we'd disrupted her one-on-one time with Mr. Hunky. I could practically hear Lilah groaning behind me.

"Shut up," I told her over my shoulder. "Tracy, get away from him."

"Is there a problem, Lissy?" Mr. Kissler asked, his voice perfectly pleasant as he stared me down. I counted slowly through the waves of nausea and concentrated on Dylan's aura.

"The problem," I said, my voice shaking and unsteady, "has a little to do with the fact that you're a murderer."

Tracy scoffed and looked at her fingernails.

Mr. Kissler laughed, a jovial and chilling sound. I shuddered, wincing at the way his Garn aura rolled slowly with the sound. "A murderer?" Listening to him, it sounded laughable, even to me.

"Linda Jones," I said, expecting him to react.

"What? That's ridiculous. She had a heart attack," Kissler said, "and right now, Tracy and I were going over some homework problems, so—"

"You weren't even doing math," Lilah pointed out bluntly from behind me. I turned to look at her, surprised. "You were trying to get her to sing for you."

"We were taking a break," Tracy told Lilah, narrowing her eyes.

A clash of the Goldens, I thought. *Interesting.*

Concentrate! my inner voice told me.

Oh yeah, I thought, *that.*

"Cody Park," I continued. Kissler's eyes opened a bit wider. "He was four years old," I said. In the back of my mind, something was nagging me, but I couldn't figure out exactly what it was. Something was a bit off.

"I don't know what you're talking about," he said. "And I'd hate to have to speak with your parents."

"I'm sure my mom would love to see you," I said. "Especially since I deactivated whatever twisted mojo you had going on in your little secret room. You think she'll recognize you? She saw Cody Park's body, you know." As the words left my mouth, it occurred to me that he must have known that.

"You went to my house?" he asked, his cool façade starting to melt away. He shook his head. "Tracy," he said, "ignore them. Sing for me."

I didn't understand it. We were confronting him with all this information, and all he wanted was for Tracy to sing to him? That just didn't make any sense, unless, of course, he was planning on killing us anyway. That was a cheerful thought.

"I don't think I feel like singing," Tracy said, her face still flushed with anger and annoyance.

"It won't hurt anything," Kissler said, his voice low and calming.

"He's lying," Lexie said suddenly, her voice louder than I'd ever heard it. I turned around to look at her. "It

223

will hurt you, Tracy." Lexie paled, and a realization settled over her face. "That's what he wants."

My mind raced. Mr. Kissler had been killing people with powers. I'd thought that maybe he was some kind of self-proclaimed witch hunter, but I was beginning to realize I was wrong.

"He wants you to sing," Lexie said again. "It'll kill you if you do."

My mind raced. What exactly did Lexie mean by that? I could feel the answer sitting in my mind, but just like on a history test, I couldn't quite access it.

"Ignore them," Mr. Kissler said to Tracy, taking her hands in his. "They're just jealous. Sing for me."

She opened her mouth.

"You're a Siren, Tracy," I said quickly, trying to break whatever spell he held over her. "Maybe you call it something else, but when you sing and concentrate on a person, you can pull them to you, make them love you."

Tracy looked at me, confused, and I wondered if she knew about her gift. What if she'd been doing it by accident? I could only imagine exactly what kind of monster she'd become if I'd just clued her into the fact that she had a magical power. She was so the type of person to use her power for evil. I forced myself to concentrate. Lexie had been right about one thing. Right now, none of that mattered. A person only saw what they wanted to see, and right now, I was seeing everything, and the Tracy-Tate thing just wasn't as important anymore.

"It's not like that," she muttered. "And how do you know this in the first place?"

"Sing," Kissler said.

Tracy looked at him, annoyed. "No," she said, her attention thoroughly fixed on me now.

He sighed and stood up. "Fine," he said, shrugging. "You girls obviously need to work something out."

As the words left his mouth, the door behind us slammed shut. I whipped around. What was going on here?

Audra tried to open the door. "It's locked," she said. "How can it be locked?"

Mr. Kissler inclined his head slightly. "Telekinesis," he said with a grin. "Courtesy of Dottie Fleming."

In that moment, everything came entirely into focus, what my mind had been hinting at all along. He wasn't just killing people with powers. He was killing them to *get* their powers. Or maybe he was stealing their powers and that just ended up killing them. Lexie had warned Tracy against singing. I had no idea how, but I knew in that instant that if Tracy had sung for Mr. Kissler, he would have stolen her gift, her voice, and Tracy would be dead right now.

And if Kissler had been willing to do that in front of us, that had to mean that he was not planning on letting us, any of us, out of there alive.

"It's sad," he said, a morose expression on his face. "So many young people dying in a fire." He shook his head and laughed, his eyes hardened, and his lips twisted into a gruesome expression that matched the awfulness of his aura. "It's even sadder that I didn't get my parting gift from Tracy first."

Tracy looked at him, outraged. "My mother," she informed him, putting her hands on her hips, "knows the governor, and when she hears about this—"

"She isn't going to hear about it," Lilah told her sharply. "You are so dense, Tracy. He's going to kill us, so Mommy dearest won't ever have anything to hear."

"What fire?" Audra asked, looking around, sounding a lot calmer than I felt.

The trash can exploded into flames, and Kissler smiled.

Dylan looked at me. "I think I know what pyrokinesis is," he said.

Kissler took a step toward me. Dylan moved to stand directly in front of me.

"You want her," he said, "you go through me first."

The teacher ignored him. "What do you see?" he asked. "When you look at me, what do you see? I know you're gifted, or at least I imagine you would be, legacy of Shannon and all that."

I stared at him, hard. "What do you know about that?" I asked. For a moment, it was as if we were the only two people in the room, each of us holding the answers to the other's questions.

"I make it my business to know," he said. "You could say it's a calling."

"What are you?" I asked.

He smiled, and all over the room, flames burned, exploding one by one as he spoke. "There are many names for what I am," he said. "Chaesmonolite if you want to get technical, Power Holder, Magnet—I think that one is particularly clever." His deadly smile deepened, and only Dylan's presence sheltered me from the full, devastating effect of his aura.

"I have the ability to take the powers of others, pull them toward my body like a magnet, and make them my own," he said. "The Holder part comes from people like me who have chosen to adopt the powers and only temporarily hold them until they can sell them. I prefer to keep them to myself."

"People like you?" I asked incredulously. "You're not a person. You're a monster."

"You say potato," he said.

"You kill people," I hissed. "Little kids who never hurt anyone."

"There are worse things," he said. "One day that *kid* you so righteously defend may discover that he has a power, may get angry. I'm not the only monster in this room. We aren't so different, you and I."

"You don't know anything about me," I said fiercely.

"No?" he asked tauntingly. The room began to fill with smoke, and I could hear the others coughing behind me. Lilah and Audra began to scream, and Lexie added her voice into the mix. I could hear someone banging on the door from the outside.

He grabbed my hand roughly in his. "Do they really look all that different?" he asked.

I looked down to see his Garn aura intertwining with the lights surrounding my hands, a prism of colors. Looking hard enough and long enough, I saw Garn in myself. It was like one of those old murder mystery movies, when the main character suddenly realizes that he's the one killing people.

I'd only seen what I wanted to see.

I shook my head, unsure of what kinds of tricks he was playing. The colors in my aura swirled, and purple came to the surface. I'd never been purple before, but I figured if there was ever a time for my bitch gene to surface, it was now.

I put my hand on his chest and shoved him backwards. "You'll die here too," I said, trying not to breathe in much smoke.

He shook his head. "Teleportation," he whispered, as if it was a secret. "A little trick I picked up from a child in Bangkok." He clicked his tongue.

"I won't let you leave," I said firmly.

"And what are you going to do about it, little girl?" he asked derisively. "That's the shame about a nonactive power like the *Sight*." His voice dripped with sarcasm on the word "Sight," and I could barely stand it. "You can see it, but you can't do anything about it."

I knew one thing. I couldn't let him out of there alive. Instinctively, my hand shot out, but this time, it wasn't my real hand. Without even meaning to, I'd come out of my body. Moving on instinct, I shoved my ghost hand into his aura, and I was pulled instantly into darkness as if I was drowning in a lake at nighttime. I couldn't breathe. Throwing out my other hand, I searched blindly, desperately for Dylan's aura, and finally, I felt the string that connected my body to his stretch until it included my astral self as well. The light between us flashed pearl, and after a moment, I could see again.

Kissler glared at my physical body. As long as I had a hold on his aura, he wasn't going anywhere. I watched with my ghost eyes as my real body fell to the ground. I wondered if my heart was still beating. I looked around the room, Dylan's aura lunged toward mine, and somehow, looking into the pearl, I felt myself start moving before my mind even realized that the rest of me had a plan. I bent down and ran my fingertips through my own aura. Like paper clips to a magnet, the prism of colors that was my aura jumped into my grip. With my own aura string in my left hand and Kissler's in my right, I glanced around the room for a minute, my vision blurred by the power of the strings that I held, jerking and moving, rebelling against my hold on them.

I saw my friends and my sister struggling against the smoke. All around them, the flames continued to explode. Kissler looked around frantically, realizing that he was trapped here. He was learning, slowly, that my power *was* an active power, and that I wasn't quite as helpless as he had thought, not that it was doing us a whole lot of good. Bringing him down with me wasn't exactly my idea of a Snoopy dance–worthy victory.

Looking around the room, I saw auras of all colors: Audra's peach, lavender from Lilah, a true purple from Tracy, pink around Lexie, and the beautiful pure white surrounding Dylan. Without thinking, I took my own hypercolor aura, which I held in my left hand, and tied it to Mr. Kissler's in my right.

On the floor, my body jerked violently, and Kissler fell to his knees. The connections fought, but for the moment, they held. Moving around the room, I grabbed blindly for more strings. First Lexie's, and from the moment her pink aura made contact with the Garn, Kissler visibly paled. My string pulled against Kissler's and Lexie's did the same, distorting the shape of his aura as the man screamed and screamed.

As Lexie shuddered under the pressure of Kissler's writhing aura, a familiar voice filled my mind.

See. Remember. Know.

Images raced through my head. *Me. Lexie. Lilah. Three intertwining circles of different colors on a silver shield. The shield of Shannon.*

See. Remember. Know.

In my mind, I could see a single aura, filled with colors as rich and varied as any aura I'd ever seen: purple, lilac, lavender, violet, light blue, pink. Color layered on top of color on top of color. The image jumped into my mind, and as surely as I'd known that Colin and Sarah would make a good match, I knew what I had to do.

Moving quickly, I ran toward Lilah. Somehow, through some cosmic blip, or possibly through Fate's desire to screw me over, she was a part of this. I stood there in front of her for a second, my astral eyes staring into her stark blue ones. After a while, she stared back, and as my hand moved toward her aura, I saw her nod almost imperceptibly. Could she see me? Did she know what I was doing?

My hand touched her aura, and as it did, a bright light flashed through the room, so quickly that I thought I'd imagined it. The sound of Kissler's screams brought my mind back to the present, and with a piece of Lilah's aura in my hand, I lunged back toward the Garn aura. I pulled and stretched and forced myself to plunge my hand into his nothing-colored aura one last time. With my teeth clenched, I tied the final knot, attaching his aura to Lilah's.

One by one, the aura strings pulled downward, stripping the Garn from Kissler's body. Pink. Purple. Blue. Lexie. Lilah. Me.

Exhausted, I fell back into my body, and then there was blissful darkness.

16

clear

Three intertwining circles, rings of different colors on a silver shield.

I looked around. "Shannon?" I said, my voice echoing in the space. I'd been here before, many times in the past week, but until this moment, I hadn't understood. I'd never wanted my dreams to be real, never wanted them to mean something.

I'd never wanted my Sight.

"I see now," I said quietly. Wind whipped gently through my hair, and I realized that this time, there was no fire in the dream, no quaking earth, no screaming walls. What was to be had come to be, and now, this place was peaceful once more.

She appeared out of nowhere, walking toward me from a distance. Her dark hair stood out against the white space, and as she walked, my eyes were drawn again and again to the three intertwining circles.

"It was my shield." Shannon's lips didn't move, but I heard her voice in my head.

"Your shield," I echoed, and I realized that I was talking without moving my lips as well.

She nodded. "The sign of my house, the heart of my line."

"He had it, there in his house," I said. She said nothing, and though no words passed between us, suddenly I understood. "He was obsessed. With you, with us. With powers in general, and in the end, it's what brought him down."

She nodded regally, her eyes locked on mine.

"I see now," I said again, my lips perfectly still. "I really do. I see everything."

"Everything, my daughter?" A soft smile played across her face. "Even the Champion? Even the lives you lived before?" Her voice was captivating, and I couldn't have looked away from her face if I'd wanted to. "You don't see everything," she said, "but you will. She has always seen, and you see, and she will see."

"Who has always seen?" I asked. After all this, there was still another mystery to be solved? I wasn't sure I could take it. "Always seen what?"

"You will see," Shannon promised. "Soon." Moving toward me, she pressed a firm kiss to my forehead. "My daughter."

From deep inside my consciousness, I heard a sound like an atomic bomb, or at least what I imagine one would sound like, and a moment later, I opened my eyes to the wailing of a fire engine.

"I've got you," a deep voice said, and I saw an image

in my mind of Dylan's strong arms closing around me, lifting me off the floor as he had staggered out the door of the burning classroom. I wondered where it had come from and decided that, deep down, I probably knew. Apparently, the First Seer was into parting gifts.

"Are you okay?" I asked him, coughing. He nodded, and a fireman rushed by.

"Lissy," my mom cried out, pain evident in her voice. When had she gotten there?

"Mom?" I said. "What's going on?"

Dylan set me down softly, and I fell into my mom's arms in a tight hug.

"I saw you in his house, saw the notes," she said, her voice breaking. "I don't know why I didn't believe you before. I should have believed you, but I just didn't."

"He had you under some kind of blindfold mojo," I said.

"Now!" I heard a familiar voice boom. I looked around to find Grams yelling at a fireman. From the looks of things, she was trying to get him to let her into the building. "That poor man is still in there," she said.

I looked at Dylan. "What happened to Mr. Kissler?" I asked.

Dylan shrugged. "He fell to the floor," he said, "and there was a loud sound, and I swear the guy exploded."

"What did you do to him?" Grams asked.

I gave her a Who, me? look, but she didn't buy it for a second.

"Jonah Kissler was a wonderful man," Grams said fiercely. She walked toward me, fury clear on her face, and as she advanced, I shrank back. She looked fit to kill. What was with her? I'd beaten the bad guy. Wasn't that what I was supposed to do?

Then I remembered. "Dylan, the picture," I said. "Do you still have the picture of Grams we found at Kissler's house?" He dug into his back pocket and handed it to me. Sure enough, the black tar substance still covered her face.

I went to scratch the tar off her face, but before I got the chance, Lexie stepped in front of me.

"He was evil," she said softly, conviction in her voice. "He was going to kill Tracy, then all of us."

The picture warmed in my hands, and I watched, openmouthed, as the tar melted away. I certainly hadn't done that. I turned to look at Lexie.

"It's true," she said. With her words, the last bit of the tar fell off the picture.

Grams shook her head as if clearing it, and then she looked at the picture and let out an inhuman whoop.

Everyone, including the firemen, stared at her.

"Fire," she said, gesturing toward the school. The firemen obeyed, jumping back to work immediately.

"A shield," she muttered, testing the tar substance with her fingers. "A magical blindfold. That little rat."

I could think of a few stronger insults, but since my mother was present, I didn't vocalize them.

Grams gathered Lexie to her in a hug. "Child, I'm so sorry," she said.

"What?" Lexie asked, looking a little uncomfortable at the fact that this was all happening in front of witnesses. A crowd had gathered in front of the school at the sound of the fire engines.

"For not recognizing your gift sooner," she said.

She has always seen.

Lexie's eyes widened, but she proceeded cautiously.

"True Vision," Grams said proudly, gesturing toward the photograph. "It's a very rare gift. Think, my pixie girl, how did you know to believe your sister?"

"It was just true," Lexie said. Then a slow and disbelieving smile spread across her face. "When she said the words, it just looked true. Everything was a little bit clearer."

"True Vision," Grams repeated. "The ability to physically distinguish the truth from a lie, and, in some cases, to make that truth evident to others, based on nothing more than how purely you believe it."

"The Sight?" Lexie whispered in awe. "I have it? Really?" She started bouncing from foot to foot, and even after what had happened today, I had to smile too. After the day we'd all had, I figured that someone deserved to be happy.

"So that's why Dylan believed you right away," I said. "You knew it was true, and that just rubbed off on him."

Lexie nodded happily. "I guess so," she said. "I just never noticed it." She wrinkled her forehead for a moment. "I don't even know when it started."

The fire chief came out to make a statement to the crowd, saying only that the classroom in question was burned beyond repair, as were several of the surrounding ones, but that the fire had ultimately been contained, and that no one was seriously injured. Whatever had happened to Mr. Kissler, he hadn't left a body behind.

"He's gone," I whispered to Lexie.

She looked at me for a minute and then nodded. "Yeah," she said. "He's gone."

"Excuse me, Mrs. James," a deep voice said, and I looked over to see a police officer talking to my mom. "I need to speak with your daughters."

"I already told you what happened," Lilah said loudly. "Mr. Kissler was in there alone with Tracy, trying to put some moves on her, and when we all showed up, he went nutso and started setting the place on fire."

I made a mental note to thank Lilah later. Whatever questions the police asked, I now knew exactly what story to tell them, and Dylan, Audra, Lexie, and, assuming she wasn't as dumb as she looked, Tracy did, too. Lilah's voice was just shrill enough that it carried.

"My mother knows the mayor, and if you don't leave me alone . . ." I heard another shrill voice shrieking. I looked toward Tracy. I knew her secret, and now, she knew at least part of mine. I was pretty sure she wasn't going to be telling anyone anything.

Finally, whatever had started with Cody Park back in California was over, and through some crazy chain of events, I'd been the one to end it, in a high school in a small town in Oklahoma.

And I'd thought there wouldn't be anything to do here.

Like so many other times in life, I'd been wrong.

17

blue again

"Close your eyes and listen to the sound of silence. Before you can see, you must learn to listen."

I tried not to pay too much attention to my grandmother's words. After all, the last time I'd let her play the magic mentor game, I'd ended up with an active power that no one in my family, not even the first Shannon, had ever had.

Once she was out from underneath Kissler's spell, Grams had listened to everything I'd had to say. She'd even given my newfound abilities a name.

"A Weaver," she'd said. "Our family has never had a Weaver."

I was satisfied. After all, "Weaver" (because I liked to think of myself as one of a kind) was a lot more cryptic than "Aura Seer." The ability to tie connections between people, to weave together lives, also came with increased responsibility. I hated responsibility, but since Colin and Sarah were still going strong (much to the dismay of the entire Golden population of Emory High), I decided that this power was worth the burden I had to bear.

Beside me, Lexie twitched. She was thrilled to be taking lessons with Grams, more so than I was, but she had too much energy for meditation just yet. She was still on cloud nine about finally getting her Sight, and the fact that she'd had it all along didn't lessen her joy one bit.

I opened my eyes. "Come on, Grams," I said. "No more meditation today. It's Saturday. I have plans."

"Plans?" a voice snorted from the doorway. "What kind of plans?"

I narrowed my eyes at Lilah. It wasn't enough that she'd invaded my dreams, my visions, my car, and my life. Now she was invading my meditation lessons.

"Look, I'm sure whatever you and your little Nontourage have planned is invigorating or whatever," Lilah said, "but my mom wanted me to check and see if you two wanted to come shopping with us tomorrow, and your mom said you guys were over here." She sounded about as thrilled to be extending the invitation as I was to get it.

"Not interested," I said shortly. Lilah and I had come to an unspoken agreement since that day with Kissler. I stayed out of her life, and she stayed out of mine, messes and all.

"Fine," Lilah said, turning immediately to leave. "See you on Monday."

Someday, I promised myself, I'd learn not to take everything she said as a threat, even if her tone of voice did sound like she was planning to sacrifice me to the altar of the rumor gods or something first thing Monday morning.

"Stay, child," Grams said, and Lilah's eyes narrowed.

"Sorry," she said. "Not interested."

Grams smiled a knowing smile, and as Lilah walked back out the front door, I found myself wishing for about the millionth time that I knew what exactly my grandmother's Sight was. Beside me, Lexie kept her eyes closed for a moment longer and then opened them.

"How did you do it?" Lexie asked, filling the silence with a question. I knew immediately what "it" she was referring to. She'd asked me the same question at least a thousand times since our brush with death, and the fact that I never had a real answer for her didn't stop her from asking. Each time, she just told me to make up an answer, because she'd know instantly whether or not it was true.

"I just tied all our aura strings to his," I said simply. "I don't know why. He said something about me being like him, and he made me see Garn in myself. Looking down and seeing that almost killed me, and I guess I just figured that if looking at my aura did that to me, maybe tying our auras to him would force him to confront his own Garn somehow."

It was the best guess I'd managed to come up with so far.

Lexie was looking at me, fascinated.

"Is that right?" I asked, trying to tap into her True Vision.

"Not exactly," she said, smiling, "but it's a whole lot closer than last time."

I shrugged. Maybe it was one of those things we'd never know the answer to, like why, ever since that day, my aura had stayed a steady baby blue. I, for one, had had enough of fighting evil and all the glorious whatnot that went with it. Lexie was still holding out for a visitation from Shannon.

Thinking of my own cryptic dreams, especially the last one, I turned to Grams, a question on my lips. "In my dreams—"

"Visitations," she corrected at high volume. She and Lexie were absolutely convinced that somehow the great First Seer in our family line had visited me in my dreams, and I hadn't even told them about the tapestry in Kissler's house.

I shrugged and started again. "In the visitations," I said, "Shannon's aura was the same color as Dylan's. That's kind of weird, isn't it?"

Grams smiled. "The Champion," she said knowingly.

The Champion. Shannon had said the same thing.

"What's that supposed to mean?" I asked.

In my purse, my cell phone rang. I ignored it, but Grams nodded her head. "Answer," she said simply.

I dug my phone out, leaving the room briefly to talk.

"Hello?" I said, expecting Audra or Dylan. The three of us had plans for a bad B-movie night.

"Hey, Lissy," a female voice said on the other end.

"Jules," I said, surprised. California seemed a lifetime away. "I haven't heard from you in a long time. What's up?" I shifted my weight, sure that this was a phone call about her latest conquest.

In the background, I heard a male voice, and I couldn't help but smile. How very like Jules to have her new Him with her when she called to tell me about Him.

When I heard a male voice on the line, I let out a small laugh. When Jules fell for a guy, she fell immediately and fell hard. Twirling a piece of hair with my fingertips, I wondered absentmindedly what her connections looked like.

"So what's his name?" I asked bluntly, knowing quite well that the guy was on the line too.

"Whose name?" Jules asked, and she paused for just long enough between the two words that my sketch-o-meter started going off.

"Your new boy's name," I said.

There was a long pause on the other line.

"Paul," Jules said finally.

"Doesn't that get confusing?" I asked. "What with Paul-Paul?"

"Lissy." The male voice on the other end of the phone stopped my babbling in a heartbeat.

"Paul." I immediately felt a stab of Tracy-like jealousy.

Don't be ridiculous, I told myself. *There's nothing to feel that way about. Paul and Jules have always hung out. It's not like there's anything there.*

Dum dum dum, my inner voice said, echoing tension-building music in a very ominous way.

I knew what Paul was going to say before he said it. "Jules and me," he said. I got the sense that he meant to say more, but he just didn't.

I opened my mouth and then closed it again. Jules and Paul? It figured. My best friend and my best guy, together. I officially sucked at life.

"Lis?" Jules said, coming back onto the line.

Not my best friend anymore, I thought.

"Lissy?" Paul repeated Jules' words.

Not my best guy anymore.

"Yeah," I said, my mouth dry.

"Are you okay?" she asked.

I wanted to ram my head into a brick wall, but other than that, I was fine.

"I'm okay," I told her. It was a lie, of course. I wasn't fine. How could I be fine? Paul and Jules. Jules and Paul. There was no world in which I would have been fine, and yet, for some reason, it just wasn't having the impact it should have.

I couldn't help but think of Dylan and Audra, Sunset Sarah, and even Lilah, Tracy, and Fuchsia. This was Oklahoma, and California—Paul, Jules, heartbreak, and all—was about a million miles away and not getting any closer.

"Listen, guys," I said, "I'm at my grandmother's. I have to go. I'll call you later."

I waited for them to say their goodbyes before I hung up the phone.

I walked back into the other room. This was it. There was no going back, not that there ever really had been. Now, there was nothing to go back to, unless, of course, I developed some burning desire to see Paul and Jules making out with each other.

Not likely.

"You were saying?" I asked Grams darkly, trying not to feel too sorry for myself. "Some cryptic nonsense about a Champion?"

Grams wisely ignored my tone. "The women in our family are Seers," she said. I curbed the urge to roll my eyes. She wasn't telling me anything I didn't already know. "The men in our family, the destined ones we bring into our family through marriage and through birth, are something entirely different."

I thought of Uncle Corey.

"A Champion, someone to help the Seer see clearly, someone to anchor them in the real world, to fight through the darkness." I listened halfheartedly to my grandmother's words.

Lexie grinned. She was liking the sound of this. "Do you have a Champion?" she asked curiously. If it could be filed under the title of Boys, Lexie was, as a general rule, incredibly interested. I, on the other hand, had just decided to swear off boys completely. Boys kissed you and then started dating your best friend the second you moved away forever and ever.

Grams smiled softly. "I did have a Champion," she said. "Your grandfather."

"Hold on there, Skippy," I said, trying not to think about the fact that I'd just addressed Grams as Skippy. "What's this have to do with Dylan's aura and Shannon's visitation?" Wasn't that what we'd been talking about before?

Grams and Lexie grinned at me like Cheshire cats. "You have got to be kidding me," I said, shaking my head. Dylan, the brooding wonder, my destined partner in life? No way. I'd just gotten dumped by someone I'd never even dated, and they were telling me that broody boy was my soul mate? That my Sight had just picked him out for me even though I so wasn't over Paul yet?

Well, my gift could just forget about it. Dylan and I were friends, and friends who annoyed each other like no other, at that. Nothing more.

Lexie and Grams kept grinning at me.

"Stop it," I told them. "There's nothing going on with Dylan and me. We just bonded over our mutual enemies."

Lexie rolled her eyes. "Lilah isn't your enemy," she told me. "And you said that Tracy has been on her best singing behavior ever since she found out you knew."

Tracy and Tate had since broken up, and Audra was scheming on the Tate front, even though she never said anything about it. "Tracy still hates me," I muttered.

"No comment," Lexie said.

"She wants me to suffer," I said. Lexie remained wisely quiet. Tracy and I had reached some kind of unspoken truce that I thought Lilah had probably had a hand in. I didn't mess with them, and they didn't go out of their way to make my life miserable. From Golden girls, I had a feeling that was about as good as I was going to get.

"I have to go," I said, picking my purse up off the floor.

"Where?" Lexie asked.

"To Dylan's," I replied without thinking.

The Cheshire cat smiles came back with a vengeance. I decided it was best to ignore the two of them. As I headed out the door to walk to Dylan's, the one thing I knew for sure was that there was *nothing* going on between the two of us.

about the author

A native Oklahoman, Jennifer Lynn Barnes is a recent graduate of Yale University. She enjoys procrastinating, gazing at shiny objects, playing with monkeys, and anything that involves volleyball and/or ballet. The closest things she has to magical powers are the ability to correctly guess the number of siblings a person has upon first meeting them and a supernatural knack for getting good parking spaces at the mall. She wrote *Golden* at the age of nineteen. Her second novel, *Tattoo,* is due out in 2007.